Also by La'Von Gittens

The Divine Apocalypse Series

Book 1: *The Beginning of the End*

Book 2: *Addiction and Clearing*

Book 3: *Attis*

Book 4: *Coming soon…*

Nonfiction

Chicken Caesar Salad For the Gay Soul

DiVINE APOCALYPSE

Addiction and Clearing

La'Von Gittens

Published by NoV'al Publishing in 2021

ISBN: 978-0-9843466-1-5 (paperback)

Published by NoV'al Publishing

www.novalpublishing.com

Prologue

"Who are we to close doors? In the early Church, even today, there is the ministry of the ostiary. And what did the ostiary do? He opened the door, received the people, allowed them to pass. But it was never the ministry of the closed door, never."
Pope Francis

The scent of cigar smoke and whiskey filled the tiny motel room so thickly it covered the furniture like poisonous dew. Agitated, even the sturdy, one-hundred and seventy-five-pound pitbull winced in the smog. Though the only window was open, it did little to filter the stagnant, hot air. Under dull and dim fluorescent lighting, Mr. Al Pike squinted and when he tapped his cigar onto the gray, stained carpet, the door opened. Instinctively he reached for the nine-millimeter attached to his waist, even though the guests were expected and right on time.

One by one, the members of the Blood Wolf Gang trickled in and threw black duffel bags onto the rickety bed frame. Weishaupt counted two suitcases and narrowed his eyes as he stirred the ice in his whiskey. Erik Lennon stumbled into the room last, late. He had off-white teeth and an unshaven brown beard. Behind him was a voluptuous young woman with skin the color of loose-leaf paper and lips the hue of raspberries.

Pike's hands rested at his hip, and he gestured toward the pale woman with long black hair and asked, "Who the hell is that?"

"She's a celebration present, boss," a crooked smile crossed Lennon's face when he spoke, "a whore I picked up off Christopher street. She don't look too bad. Not that beat up. You'll like her, b-because we think you're going to be very happy with what we got." The older man nodded sarcastically as he unzipped the first two travel bags.

Cash.

Stacks of it.

"How much?" Pike inquired as he raised an eyebrow.

"Six-hundred-and-thirty-five thousand," Holmes cleared his throat and answered hesitantly. New to the Blood Wolves, Holmes was unsure of their missions and had yet to get paid. Nervously he asked, "You think Fire Giant will let us take a cut?"

Unimpressed, he unzipped the third bag.

It was stuffed with jewelry. Without breaking a stance, Pike filled his lungs with his cigar. Densely, he planted his weight back onto the squeaky motel room chair. The three men before him exhaled so loudly the room grew warmer.

"Were you followed?" Pike slanted his gaze and asked with a coil of suspicion in his voice.

"No, s-sir," Lennon stuttered.

"Then let the games begin," Pike announced, opened his arms, and spread his legs as the men cheered in relief.

Lennon tossed the black-haired woman to the gang leader.

Diamond Love quivered as she fell to her knees before the heavyset man. Her hazel eyes rolled as her lips curved up with a grimace. Slightly disgusted, she informed them, "Old guys are extra."

"Just do your job; you'll get paid," Pike frowned as he instructed.

"Okay," she agreed, then licked her lips. Her nostrils expanded as her heart sped. Pike unzipped his pants, but her focus was torn. In the corner of her eye, a glimmer led to the open duffel bag, particularly a silver ring. She was suddenly nervous; there was a sour taste in her mouth. Diamond quivered but could not force her gaze off the ring that sat on top of the open sack.

The lump of metal was nothing special. It had no expensive gems or rare crystals. There was only a symbol that reminded her of a Jewish star. Her bottom lip trembled as she almost lost sight of it. Completely enthralled, she lifted a hand to it. Just as her four-inch ruby red nails touched the bag, Pike cleared his throat disapprovingly.

"You like it?" he raised an eyebrow when he asked as she slowly nodded. "Take it. Consider it your payment for our entertainment. Come on now, first me, then my dogs."

"Really?" Lennon chuckled, "That cheap old thing?"

What had come over her? She was confused but determined. Like a starved animal unleashed, she darted toward the bag and slipped the ring on her right index finger. Immediately her heart slowed as fresh water ran through her blood, and her brain lit up with electricity.

It smelt like burnt marshmallows.

Diamond Love was in a room full of dirty men. They cooked cocaine, laughed, and counted the money. She swallowed a rock in her throat and looked down at Mr. Pike and his exposed privates.

Instinct quickly took over. Diamond was a seasoned professional. She tucked her long straight hair behind her ear and looked Pike directly in the eye. Diamond bit her lower lip and took a handful of his throbbing body. Without breaking eye contact, she bent over and serviced him as the spectators in the background hooted like hyenas.

At this point, she was an expert. Within moments she was finished. Her long black extensions covered her face like hairy tarantula legs, and she wiped her mouth clean. Diamond's eyes rolled into the back of her head. "Alright, who's you got next? I can't be fucking with y'all all day…"

"For this one," Pike announced as he finished his whiskey, "he needs you to take off that cheap dress."

She exhaled loudly and gently pulled off her strapless zebra print skirt. Her shape was unreal and so well manufactured that her proportions defied gravity. Diamond bit her plump lower lip in impatience.

"Get in the bed," he commanded with such authority Diamond Love was inclined to follow. He inched on top of her and held her wrists above her head to treasure the moment. Pike reached his hand above her ears and revealed the bondage that was attached to the bed. Like he had done this many times before, he strapped in her arms and legs before she realized what was happening around her.

Diamond never showed fear. She grunted in her restraints and refused to break her gaze with Pike. She spat through false bravery, "Alright, I feel you. You guys are freaky, huh? You like it when a girl is tied up?"

"Not us," a twisted smile curved around Pike's lips as he admitted, "him."

Pike rolled off the woman as his crew dropped the pit bull on top of her like a warm sack of mud. The overweight canine slobbered so profusely that the sticky liquid dripped from his jaws and melted down Diamond's exposed nipples. His golf ball brown eyes connected with hers as she could feel the animal begin its motion.

"Argh!" Diamond cried out but could not escape the binds. "H-hold up! I didn't sign up for this!"

"I did say me then my dogs, right?" Pike confirmed, letting loose a bellowing laugh, and his teammates joined him in amusement.

Diamond's mind went blank again. She reached out for something to grab. Anything. She struggled to move but failed to budge. Panic strangled her as the pitbull groaned. It was almost as though she had an out-of-body experience. Her right hand dug into the wooden bed frame so intensely her long red fingernails broke off. One by one, they fractured and revealed five bloody nubs as she screamed.

She felt the pain, every nerve in every digit, but her hand was not her own. As if controlled by another being, her hand moved faster than her thoughts ever could.

Something cracked.

Diamond held the dog up by its throat. Her grasp was so tight the animal could barely whimper.

Her eyes widened as she snapped the pitbull's neck as quickly as she would turn a doorknob. Lennon screamed, and the men shouted obscenities behind him. Involuntarily, with the same free hand, she grabbed Pike by the belt buckle and dragged him to the ground. With the speed that outmatched the accomplished mobster, Diamond Love swiped the gun from his waist and pointed it at the frightened men.

Air rushed into her enlarged chest. Diamond's eyes were saucers of water, and she shook as though she had no idea what she was doing. Her free hand, however, pointed the gun without a waiver.

"U-unstrap me."

"Chill…" Lennon cautioned as he unzipped the binds on her legs. Defeated, he raised his arms and hesitantly unlocked her left arm. "Just get out of here, you crazy ho…"

Unable to form a thought, Diamond wrapped herself up in the maroon sheets to cover her nudity. In total shock, she struggled to inch off the bed when Pike grabbed her by the ankle. With an assassin's expert movement, Diamond fired a round directly between the older man's eyes.

Suddenly she was hypersensitive. Things were in slow motion. Diamond had done terrible things in her life, but she had never murdered anyone.

"You stupid ho!" Lennon shouted as he attacked her with a switchblade.

Caught completely off guard, Diamond tumbled and was slashed across the thigh. Her body was weak, but her right hand swerved with the agility of a soldier. Two rounds later, Lennon was dead.

She scrambled to her feet and almost tripped on his blood in the process. For a moment, Diamond begged her arm to stop, but in an instant, the two remaining men were down. Dead.

She dropped the gun.

Her arm was back under her control. Diamond gazed at her right hand as though it were a stranger as tears melted off her makeup. This was a cheap motel, but someone was bound to hear the noise. Apprehensively, she slipped back on her zebra print dress. She turned toward the door but paused in mid-step. It took a moment, but she rushed to the suitcases. Diamond stuffed as much as she carried into two duffel bags and threw them over her shoulder before she rushed through the door.

Copper scents of lukewarm blood and rotting flesh sluggishly filtered out of the motel room. Hours later and no one had discovered the horrific scene beside the flies that buzzed in through the open window. Like dead fish on display, the twisted men were frozen in horror—jaws open and eyes clouded. Echoes of tiny humming wings bounced off the walls as the flies feasted on the banquet before them.

The two men remained unmoved by the gruesome scene but became disappointed as they examined the room. Walt Excel was a four-and-a-half foot middle-aged man with a round body and messy blonde hair that came out of the sides of his head in stubborn patches. A white and gray mink robe draped over his stocky shoulders and covered his large platinum necklace that rested on his hairy chest. He didn't wear a shirt but had silk socks and seal skin loafers. A long frown wiggled across his wrinkled lips when he sulked, "Well now, looks like we're too late!"

"It appears so," the second a man sighed.

"Don't we usually send people to do this sort of stuff for us?" Walt asked. He shook his head regrettably and admitted, "Gatherin' dees things, can't we find someone to do it for us? For you know… cheap?"

"I wanted to gather this one personally," he cleared his throat before he spoke. "Sometimes, I get bored in that big old spa."

"I guess the element found its ahhhh…" Walt waved his finger aimlessly as he struggled to find his words, "its human or whatever. Now it ain't the end of the world. We got the resources. We'll get that ring in no time. It's just one pesky human."

"That's not what I'm worried about," Hubbard Bainbridge sighed and realigned his checkered sweater.

"Aw, come on now!" Walt's southern accent wrestled his tongue when he spoke, "You still worried about him? We'll always be brothers! God damn Princes of Hell, that's who we are!"

"I just like my family the way it is," Hubbard Bainbridge said as he shut his eyes in reminiscence. "We don't need to add anyone else to it."

"But change is good; change can be more lucrative," Walt disagreed but smirked. "He could help us."

"Thank you for trying to help." Defeated Bainbridge's shoulders sunk. "But please be quiet before I rip out your tongue and choke you with it."

Walt hesitated for a moment then held his jiggling stomach as he chuckled, "Let's go find your ring."

Water. Hair gel. Butter. She could not take the ring off. She could not sleep. Diamond had spent the day pacing in her cramped motel room; she had to get out, but there was nowhere for her to go. Except for work. She was the first girl in the locker room and had time to pace time back and forth. Every sound frightened her. The money and the jewelry were tightly packed in her closet, but somehow, she could feel the green paper and precious stones on her skin. Her brain was a watery stew with the little notion. Imagination haunted her as she could almost sense the money behind the door laugh at her.

Diamond was still bleeding. Her thigh itched as she bit the long red nails on her left hand.
Annoyed, she fetched a first aid kit from the locker room bathroom. The ivory-skinned woman sat on the sticky bench

and emptied the bag's contents onto her unwashed beach towel. It was like she spilled a bucket of loose Legos.

Nothing looked familiar. She picked up a half-used tube of burn cream. Her wound burned, so it did seem appropriate.

As she opened the tub, she suddenly felt a tickle in her right hand. Her jaw dropped as each digit moved independently. Her hand threw the burn cream aside. In awe, she watched as her arm moved with a mind of its own. It opened the disinfectant wipes and started to clean the wound on her leg. It stung a little, and Diamond winced. Stunned, she figured it was best just to let the hand do what it wished. Part of her wanted to get up and run, but she had nowhere to go. No one to care for her. Her right hand opened the antibiotic cream and applied it to her wound. The almost alien hand cleaned and bandaged her wound like a vigilant nurse. She looked at her appendage and wondered if she had gone mad as it moved with a knowledge that she was ignorant to.

It was only 6:47 pm, and the club had just opened, but Diamond was so jittery that she needed to get her mind off things. She took a bump of the coke from the batch she had stolen the night before. Disappointed, she focused on work. Before she walked to the dance floor, she stopped by the mirror to check herself. Even though she was terrified, she looked gorgeous.

Jet black hair mixed with weave extensions draped down to her pierced belly button and over her black lace bra and panties. She wore fishnets and high leather heels, but her favorite piece was her new platinum and ruby necklace she had stolen from the motel's men. She was sure to make money tonight because it brought all the attention to her breasts.

"Where were you last night?" Daddy Knigge snarled as he entered the locker room. "You never checked in."

"You didn't call me, okay?" Diamond defended herself then fell back when her lungs filled with hot air.

"What is that?" he asked as the pimp snatched the necklace off Diamond's throat. "You freakin ho. Where did you get this? You been holding out on me?"

"No, I ain't holding out on you, Daddy," Diamond spat defensively. "It was a gift."

"Nobody gives hos gifts," the Asian man commanded and put the necklace into his pocket. "Now, get onto the stage. We have guests waiting…"

The beat of the house music suffocated the clatter of Diamond's high heels. Boldly she pranced out onto the stage and flipped her long dark mane. There were only two men in the audience. One was wearing a fur coat, and the other was dressed more like Mr. Rogers. Diamond took the metal pole into her hands then reached for her toes.

"Listen, brother," Walt Excel reasoned, "you gotta at least hear him out. Might like what the man has to say."

Brother Hubbard Bainbridge shook his head and retorted, "You know, I'm just not entirely convinced we need to sully our secret circle with the likes of an outsider. Do you really think we can trust him?"

"Hush now," Walt whispered, then leaned forward, and his attention drew to the stage, "I think this is your girl."

"I believe so," he agreed once he stood up and walked to the stage as Walt followed.

"You'd think the ring would have chosen someone," Walt supposed then shrugged, "I don't know, classier?"

They stared at her.

"Isn't it supposed to be a-a-a-a," he waved his finger around aimlessly as he tried to find his words, "a force of good and *Jesus* and all that bullshit they say around these parts?"

Diamond crossed her legs and swung up the pole like an acrobat. Once she was at the top, she unbuckled her bra and dropped it to the ground. Brother Hubbard Bainbridge flushed slightly. He reached into his pocket and politely slid three dollar bills onto the black stage.

"Erhm," Walt cleared his throat. As though he were slightly appalled, he slid the cash off the stage and put it into his wallet. "You ready to kill her?"

The exotic dancer slid down the pole like a snake on a tree. She snatched her bra up from the ground and spat at the two men, "You guys are jerks."

Offended, she exited the stage.

Diamond pinned the back of her bra together and released a massive deep breath. Daddy Knigge's nostrils flared with rage, and the vein in his forehead was popping out. It was the steroids; they made him twitchy and more agitated than usual. She knew that she had to be gentle when he was like this. But this time, he had a right to be angry.

Diamond planted her heels and looked up to the much taller man. She explained, "Those guys are broke! They out there playing games. I'm not about that mess."

"You're about whatever the hell I tell you, ho!" the pimp educated her. Then he launched.

Once he was close, Diamond felt a familiar tingle in her hand. Her right arm moved with the swiftness of a ninja and dragged her body around like a disobedient child. Diamond could barely keep up in the heels, but her fist struck out and slung her around as it did. With three quick jabs to the stomach, the groin, and the nose, the hand wrapped itself around Daddy Knigge's neck.

She forced him onto the wall and silently begged her arm not to snap this man's neck like it did the dog's just a few hours before. The man wiggled like a baby bird in her hand. Tears crept at the corner of her eyes. Now, no amount of pretending could protect her ego.

She was afraid.

"Am I sensing stage fright?" Brother Bainbridge announced while he and Walt Excel entered the locker room. "I must say, that is a shocker, coming from you."

"W-what are you stupid?" Diamond choked. "Get out of here before you get yourselves hurt."

"Oh, we're not afraid of pain," Brother Bainbridge snickered as he approached her. "And I could sense that you're not either. Strange how we can sense that about one another. How, when you're connected to someone, you can just feel it right away."

"I ain't nothing like you!" she spat as her grip grew tighter around the man's neck.

"Well, I disagree." Bainbridge placed his hands in his pockets and rocked back and forth on the heel of his shoes, "I know that deep down, you want to kill him, but you're afraid. He hurt you, didn't he? He hurt you so much you stopped feeling pain. Or so you thought. You still feel pain, my friend. But you don't have to be afraid of it. Embrace it. Take it out on him."

"You don't know what I can do," Diamond trembled when she spoke, the man in her grasp still alive.

"I know. That thing on your hand," Bainbridge grinned warmly, "has changed your life. It's called the Ring of Solomon. I can show you how to use it. Just don't be afraid you have to make a choice. Let go."

Her arm was weakening. Diamond knew she could not hold Knigge for much longer. Her right hand's job was to protect her, but it was not a killer. She needed to make that decision. With her left-hand, Diamond forced her long red nails into Knigge's eyes. The man shrieked out in horror, and Diamond pressed as deeply as she could. It was not until she was knuckled deep into the man's forehead did he fall silent. She pulled out two bloody fingers and dropped his lifeless body to the ground, "How about that?"

Brother Bainbridge glazed over to Walk and smirked. After a moment, he looked back to Diamond and offered, "Are you looking for a job, young lady?"

Chapter 1: Who Am I?

"Never regret yesterday. Life is in you today and you make your tomorrow."
L. Ron Hubbard

"Fight," Neil coached himself through the sharp, sour taste of his own vomit. Coils of pain thrashed about his insides and tightened as if he had starved for months. His migraine felt like a railroad spike to the temple, and his knees buckled like he held a thousand pounds. He felt no gravity, saw no color, but the howl of the winds was as deafening as crashing skyscrapers.

Air was bitter and froze to the bone. Everything was dark, but Neil felt the universe. Minuscule, he was the plankton that quivered in a harsh, endless sea. He was as empty as he was lost. Was this how it felt to be without God's love? Was this how it was to fall?

Bold throbs clouded his senses, yet he began to see the broken pews and smashed lights through the fogged edges of his sight. Massive crosses on the walls and stained glass windows shaped like saints were above the ripped-up tiles of the church he had defeated the White Horseman. He was still in the Jesus is Salvation Church.

Neil cringed to the cries around him. Aurora, Ezekiel, and Amanda crouched in agony just feet away. Their earsplitting wails bounced through the tall ceilings. Like flies whose wings were carelessly torn off by a child, it felt as though their limbs were plucked from them, one by one.

Thoughts refused to form as if his soul was carved out, and there was nothing but a chalky, hollow void. Misery. Was this all there was to life? Gutted from the inside out, Neil joined his crew in yelps of desperation.

Neil took in fistfuls of his vomit-stained jeans as the walls and floors vibrated with an intensity much more potent than anything he could muster. The large wooden cross fell from the entrance of the church. A shadow grew from the corners until the entire room was coated in darkness.

Adrenaline rushed through Neil's veins, and he stood as a human-shaped figure formed out of pure white light. Standing almost made him faint, but he raised his hands defensively. His fists had never seemed so heavy.

Seconds seemed like hours, and it took Neil eons to form words, but just as he cracked his lips, a white brightness emerged from above him. He looked up to see an unnatural, fluorescent glow enter through the ceiling. The beam was targeted and controlled like the stage lights of a Broadway show.

It highlighted Aurora. Slowly, she lifted off her feet. Ezekiel then Amanda. Neil gritted his teeth in anticipation and aimed an open palm at the figure made of the brightness before him, but as the white light hit, he was paralyzed. He, too, floated away helplessly.

Blackness made sight impossible, but the jury's bodily heat and warm breath made it known that this private assembly was full of spectators. Each member arrived alone and was guided to their seat by spiritual directions. The Princes of Hell knew each other deeply, but they had to honor this sacred tradition.

The Hidden Eye was a body of influentials and world leaders. For centuries they kept dangerous secrets and orchestrated devilish deals. In ivory, pyramid masks, and white cloaks, each silently hurried to their seats as no one would dare be late.

Once all were seated, a beam from the ceiling highlighted the center of the large circular table, where a baby goat awoke from its slumber. In a haze, the dwarf animal took to his feet. Like a toy on a string, it stumbled to the closet masked juryman, turned his back to him, and lifted his tail. With darkness as a cover, each assembly member kissed the goat's anus.

The kid moved counter-clockwise and stopped at each member. One by one, they pledged their loyalty by lifting their masks and kissing the goat's bare end. After the rounds were completed, the animal walked back into the center of the table. He warmed himself in the white light, curled into a ball, and shut his black oval eyes.

The flap of mighty wings echoed. A fat barn owl appeared from the darkness, and in a vicious charge, the bird ripped at the goat's throat. Savagely, the large owl tore into the baby animal with the skill of a starving butcher. The kid cried. Leathery red skin was tossed about as the goat bled to death on the black metal table.

The owl threw its head back and swallowed chunks so thick you could see the pieces travel down the bird's throat. Yellow, moon-like eyes surveyed the assembly around him as he fiercely devoured his offering so viciously that its face was red in seconds.

"You cannot deny my word," the Hallowed One smiled, wagging a wrinkled finger at the demonic audience. He was the only one who was not seated, and the spotlight was on him.

In a raspy voice, he continued, "As it is written, as it shall be. Whoever kills the Horsemen becomes the Horsemen. I have embedded the Alpha Omega with the curse of the Four Horsemen of the Apocalypse. Soon, they are under my control and will submit to any of my commands. However, I've run into a bit of an issue."

"Come on, man!" Walt chanted beneath his mask, "I was rooting for you."

"Their spirits are strong," he admitted. "Before I can fully instant the essence of the Horsemen of the Apocalypse, I have to gut their humanity. As a God of the Dead, that isn't exactly my forte."

"How do we know you actually have complete control over them?" a man with a sloppy black triangle painted on his white mask spoke.

"These juiced-up angels aren't the regular kind, you know?"

"Have faith in the poor man," Walt adjusted his robes but spoke lowly behind his milky disguise. "You've hardly given him a shot. He's the Grim Reaper, Hades, Anubis; he is no stranger to history. The power of the Alpha Omega and the Horsemen of the Apocalypse could have endless possibilities!"

"You both have valid points," a woman spoke. She calmly articulated every word with a gesture of her pale boney hands as not to upset any of the powerful men seated, "To be fair, I think that we should take a vote."

"This is supposed to be a very exclusive organization," Brother Bainbridge muttered to himself.

"Now, I know he's the Lord of the Dead, and I congratulate him on that, but I wasn't as worried about the Alpha Omega before, and I'm not now. Angel-human hybrid; they're Nephilim with souls. Disgraces! They were young, weak. They're going to get themselves killed. Were you worried?" He looked out to the table, "I'm more concerned about property taxes."

"We're the Hidden Eye. We control the world. I was never worried," the billionaire warned, a white cloak tensed around his muscular ebony arms. He fisted his meaty fingers that were covered in Super Bowl championship rings. "I just don't do well with competition. If we help you, what's in it for us?"

Hades the Hallowed One dipped his Amish hat and confirmed, "Everyone knows that the Princes of Hell are in search of certain rarities. Ankusha, Járngreipr, Aegis, Excalibur… Once the Horsemen are under my control, I can help you find them."

"And who is to say you just won't keep them for yourself?" a voice interrupted.

"I think we should do it. I heard one of them is cute. And if Nathaniel Robinson actually becomes president, it might be nice to have super-powered angel horsemen to back us up... If we're ever going to bring Hell to Earth," a younger woman was heard saying.

"We can't trust them," the first man who spoke continued loudly. "They're not like normal angels. They have souls, and if those souls ever come to the forefront, we could be resting on a huge problem."

"So, what do you suggest?" someone called out.

"They must be cleared, cleared of their humanity, their Enochian histories, and their past lives. I can take them." Bainbridge cleared his throat. "This is my territory. I'm the Highest Operating Psychic in the West Hemisphere, and I will be able to destroy what is left of humanity in those beings."

"And what of the Anti-Christ?" the younger woman voiced concern.

Chapter 2: Why Can't I Stop?

> As I looked, behold, a stormy wind came out of the north,
> and a great cloud, with brightness around it, and fire flashing
> forth continually, and in the midst of the fire, as it were
> gleaming metal.
> **Ezekiel 1:4**

Untamed weeds bathed in the sun and boldly sprouted purple and yellow flowers in their triumph over the unkempt lawn. Infused with summer energy, bindweed vines crawled from the bushes and strangled chipped statues and crumbled gravestones. Wild ivy curled around the church's massive black gate and circled the large sign that read, "Closed For Repairs."

Biff adjusted his navy suit jacket as he ignored the notice. He trotted up the cracked concrete stairs that tiny plants and anthills overran. Dust cluttered the stained glass windows so thickly that it was hard to see through. It was clear that the church had not been used for a while and was in no hurry to change.

When his knocks on the front door went unanswered, the attractive dark-skinned man strolled around the massive building. Squirrels and pigeons that had long gotten comfortable scurried away as he approached the rectory entrance and repeatedly rang the doorbell.

Excited birds squawked and fluttered into the warm summer air, and territorial wasps guarded their nests, but as far as Biff could tell, there was no movement behind the thick oak door. Slowly he knocked as he called, "Sister! I know you're in there! I'm not a bill collector or an angry Christian! Trust me!"

Stale food particles and soot floated through the air. Though it was the middle of the day, the lights were shut off, and the curtains shaded any sunlight. Dried potions used to paint the archaic protective symbols on the walls smelled like garlic and sage. Tiny bones, charms, and cloaking amulets hung from the walls and ceilings in small brown sacks covered in spider webs and mold. How did he find this place? It was supposed to be warded.

The small closet in the cluttered living room was filled with outdated computer screens and grimy file cabinets.

Stolas, the Maniae, twitched his gray head to the side as his pea-sized black eyes tried to make sense of what played before him. The small owl anxiously pecked the elderly nun's shoulder.

Nervously, Sister Lyssah Tabbris Rhamiel twisted her knotted gray hair into a braid, arched up in her squeaky chair, and wheeled herself closer to the monitor. The built man in a tight striped suit pounded on her front door. Her wrinkled fingers adjusted the volume to her computer, and Biff's voice boomed through her speakers, "Don't worry. I'm just looking for my wife! Her name is Aurora Haith! Her mother told me I might find her here. Do you know where she is? I heard she's been here!"

Hot gusts carried blackened ashes through the thick air. Fumes of sulfur stank like rotten eggs and fogged the compact wooden room. Unbearable heat and echoes of a boiling ocean radiated off the glass doors so heavily that it made them bounce. A bead of sweat rolled down his sticky forehead, and Neil's eyes burst open. Blinded by direct light, the angel cringed in agony. He gasped but choked on the gases that rose from the wooden planks on the floor. As if struck by lightning, Neil leaped from the pine bench and breathlessly slammed himself against the locked glass exit.

He was trapped in a sauna and paralyzed by the white fluorescent lights that blinded him when he gazed at them too long. Milliseconds went by like hours. Where was he? His breath made clouds on the glass, and when the brightness dimmed, he could read the bright blue logo against the white wall outside his cage, "Welcome to Obelisk House, Dianetic Hospital & Spa," then under it in red, "The Volcano Room." The words were structured inside a pyramid emblem with an eye drawn in the middle.

He recognized the name from an article he had read weeks ago; the spa was a luxury resort that few were lucky enough to afford. But this was unlike any spa Neil had ever seen. Naked and feeble, he sensed that his heartbeat in his throat. Delirium wrestled with his sound mind as he took in the horrible scene beyond his prison.

Senses clocked in one after the other, and as his dizziness subsided, he realized he was trapped in a heated sweatbox designed like a hellish sauna. Outside the glassy exit were horrors like he had never witnessed. Defenseless, he fell to his knees and placed a hand on the frosted doors.

Pale and dwarfed, skinless critters scurried around the spa beyond Neil's jail cell. Each had large, oval, charcoal-colored eyes, like nocturnal rodents. Every four-foot tall creature moved with the accuracy and purpose of a roach in an empty kitchen. Bug-like, their movements were robotic, dull, and ticked with instant inclination.

Among the shorter alien-like creatures walked sensuous beasts dressed in tight nurse uniforms. They had bodies of shapely women but scaled faces with tiny sharp teeth that were covered in blood. Each held a long surgical needle in their right hands and herded the smaller monsters like sheep as they marched like drunk prostitutes.

Minced organs filled a fountain that bubbled over in the center of the room. Red and purple, the viscera mixed with tones of gray and green as some human body parts were more diced than others. The grease boiled like cooked vomit, then the angel cringed and held his stomach in disgust.

When he touched his skin, a sour twinge rang through him. Maybe this was Hell. Thick layers of sweat covered his sliced upper body, and he realized he was completely naked.

Vulnerable and shellshocked, he covered himself with his fingers. The heat alone could make him pass out. Where was he? Neil focused on the glass doors and tried to remove them telekinetically.

Nothing.

Something was wrong. Something made him weak. He looked up to the blinding white light above him. There was a life-sucking force about it. Was he left to burn here for the rest of eternity?

No.

Neil refused to surrender.

He was weaker than he had ever been, but he knew his power was still there. His fists clenched so hard his hands crumpled. If ever there was a time to lose control, it would be now.

"Is this Hell?" the angel bellowed as if he was speaking to an actual person. "If it is, you're not going to keep me! I swear I'll kill everyone here!"

Energy gradually thickened and snapped in sparks. Neil could feel the wooden walls of the sauna shake under his psychic surge. As the pine planks beneath his feet cracked and jumped like popcorn, he summoned every ounce of strength he had left.

A crack ran down the glass door.

It was as though all of the gray dwarfs suddenly awoke from their mechanical trance. Instantly, the skinless monsters flew toward him. Neil's eyes filled with blackness. A dozen creatures approached his cell and opened the glass door.

He squinted.

Four of the trolls detonated like paper bags filled with air. Red and green fluids splashed across Neil's face. He spits a glob of blood out of his mouth. However, others moved too quickly for Neil to grab telekinetically. The child-sized demons tackled Neil with unworldly strength. His body crumpled, and his powers were more challenging to use than ever.

"Touch me, and it will be your last!" Neil shouted through full swallows of hot air. "I will not be controlled!"

The monsters overwhelmed him. With the power of his mind, Neil banished the demons who held his arms and legs. However as quickly as he crushed the pumpkin-headed gray creatures, four more entered the room as replacements.

"I'll tear this whole building apart!" Neil bellowed as the room began to shake. Where was everyone? Has the world ended? The chestnut-haired angel was void of thought but filled with the instinctual need to survive. Like surges of electricity, thunderous bolts of purple, black and gold extended from his shoulder blades. He rose six feet from the ground. With the twirl of his hand, the mighty angel cleared his pathway of the gray goblins.

He dropped to the floor.

Without wings or glowing eyes, Neil stumbled out of his holding jail and through
the hallway. Corners of his eyesight blurred still. Shoeless, he felt every pebble and detail to the ground as he navigated this new district.

Neil hobbled to the elevator. Six floors down and he was in the basement. Expressively, he gathered his strength.

The Obelisk House, Dianetic Hospital & Spa was a parlor made for the devil. Caked with layers of old blood, floral peach wallpaper surrounded displays of human bones with still fresh tendons, along with decorative white candles and phallic ivory sculptures.

The angel made a run for the staircase.

No alarm rang as he pushed through the emergency doors; nevertheless, a seemingly prepared team of four was ready to introduce themselves.

"Welcome to Obelisk House," the delicate man at the top of the stairs set conversation into motion.

Immediately, an identical gentleman below him followed the stream of consciousness, "Are you staying with us? Do you have an appointment?"

"First and last name?" a small-framed man rushed his words as he looked up to the others. They all had bright blue eyes and ear-length, black haircuts. In unison, the quadruplets placed a hand on their hips and raised their right eyebrows.

Neil was weak, naked, and fed up. He pressed his strength onto the railing and dragged himself forward. These men did not scare him. His eyes began to fill with black.

"Neil Qin, I see," one of the identical quadruplets grinned as he spoke. "Your reservation is still active. I'm going to have to escort you back to your room."

"Try it!" Neil warned, then wove an arm and launched an attack that pinned all four clones to the walls behind them. As he made it to the next level, the door was open, but the entire scenery had changed.

At the front desk of the five-star resort sat a fifth member of the very same team Neil had just defeated. The young man crossed his tall and thin legs as the blue eyes in his head rolled backward. With a hiss, he plowed the telephone into its base. Pale, with a feminine undercurrent, he flipped a lock of his dark eyebrow-length hair, took a deep breath, and surveyed the next customer with prestigious standards.

Angrily, Jackie Adams was at the front desk with a face like a cheese-less pizza. The reporter leaned in and retorted through gritted teeth, "I have to film tomorrow morning; my face is too red! You better fix this! I swear I know people! You know Sylvia Goldenblatt? She's a judge and a good friend of mine. She loves a good lawsuit!"

"Ma'am, we cannot control how your skin would react to the treatment," he sassed and continued as though he was sick of repeating himself. "That's genetics. But we do have packages that include temporal skin restoration after a peel." He folded his arms beneath a thin white vest above his black tuxedo pants, "You just haven't purchased it… If you like, I can just charge the card we have on file…"

"Argh!" Neil screamed out as he crawled out onto the lobby floor. "S-S Somebody help me!"

The nude man tried to stand, "I need some… I need some… get me out of here! Please, I need some help!"

Neil glanced out onto a room full of patient clients. Each covered their eyes and increased the volume on their headphones. In New York, naked crazed people were a temporary but common annoyance.

"Neil?" Jackie shook her head as she approached him in his delirium. "What are you doing?"

"J-Jackie?" His legs were like gelatin. Frail, Neil was oblivious bait to his surroundings. Tears dropped from his eyes, and he cried like a child.

Desperately, Neil lunged forward into the extravagant lobby.

"Please," he begged.

"Are you crazy?" Jackie asked. "Put some clothes on when you're in public! What's wrong with you?"

Neil struggled, but there were no open ears. The crowd continued as though this New York City meltdown was something witnessed daily. Neil screamed, "Someone pay attention! Call the cops… Help me!"

The blood in his veins ran ice cold. A silver ring was placed at the base of his spine, and it controlled his movements like a string did a marionette. As if he had been hit with a taser, Neil was paralyzed and forced upright.

"If I turn this ring so slightly to the left," the raven-haired woman muttered, "it will snap your spine."

"Anesthesia!" the young man quickly apologized to the crowd. "Our deepest apologies; some patients respond differently than others."

"Diamond," the thin-framed man snarled as he rose from his comforting leather chair at the front desk, "I thought you all were taking care of your clients… and that I would not have to get involved! I have enough to do around here, you know?"

"Loosen that thong in your tight ass; he just needs a little more time in the lights to drain his power," Diamond ordered, then took Neil by the back of the shoulders. "Focus on the front of the house, Tristan. I got the back…"

"We have guests here. Watch your fucking language," Tristan Bainbrige snapped through his straight white teeth.

"Okay… Neil, if you remember this, hit me up later; we have some unfinished business." Jackie breathed heavily as she retreated into the hallway but ignored the nude man, "Charge whatever you want. You people are a fucking scam anyway."

Like a lion would grab her cub, Diamond hoisted Neil by the back of his neck and forced him into the elevator.

Tristan released a heavy breath, and he regarded the next customer, "Welcome to the Obelisk House, Dianetic Hospital and Spa. Are you staying with us, or do you have an appointment? To better assist you, can I have your first and last name?"

"I'm Clara," the young girl whipped her neck and spoke with an intimidating conviction. "Might be fun to work here or whatever… You guys hiring?"

Like a cat with a mouse trapped in a box, Diamond playfully shoved Neil around the elevator. She bit her finger and licked her long red nails. Diamond was the full embodiment of sex appeal, dressed in skin-tight leather garments and boots with six-inch heels. She threatened him but was as alluring as she was arresting.

Diamond looked Neil up and down as she nibbled on her long ruby claws that were only on her left hand, "So you're Michael, huh? 'One who is like God' in human form? The most powerful angel on Earth? Of course, you picked a good body… What the Hell use is a Heavenly being without a big dick?"

"Let me go," Neil submitted. "I don't want to kill you. W-we can do this however you want…"

"We're watching the same show over here, Angel-Wings? You'll do whatever I want anyway." Diamond shrugged as the elevator doors opened. The dark-haired warrior took Neil by the chestnut locks and catapulted him back into the basement, where he sat back in his cell. He waited an hour until two other figures arrived.

"So this is the powerful Michael?" the voice was steady and articulate with the confident accuracy of a sniper shot to a turtle. Neil's heart fell into his stomach as the creature made his appearance. A chill ran down Neil's spine. Somehow Neil knew the light depleted his abilities, and he could not attack as he usually would. He raised his hands, but he was disabled as three dwarf monsters held him to the ground.

Brightness from the blazing skylight reflected off the man's balding head. He was a neat gentleman, middle-aged and charmingly plump. Clean cut, he wore an immaculate red sweater over a white button-up and blue tie. His smile was warm and friendly despite the gruesome scene of walking demons and boiling viscera that played out behind him. He greeted, "Welcome to my Dianetic Hospital, my friend; we make life changes here!"

To his left stood the Hallowed One, dressed in his usual black Amish hat and a dark suit that was too big for his thin, frail body. He smiled through a mouth full of gray teeth and confirmed, "Yes, this is Michael. 'Who is like God'… Doesn't seem like much. But he did destroy my White Horseman. I wonder how. I trained him… from the moment he entered his human body."

"They are the Alpha Omega," the man in the red sweater moved like a ghost as he spoke. "'God's fist's,' having dominion over life, thought, matter, energy, and time. I'm excited to have you here! I'm so glad that you thought of me."

"Here you are, Brother Bainbridge," like a decrepit, the Hallowed One pressed all of his energy on his cane and continued. "Clear them by any means so that they can be filled with my children. They are fighting against our influences…They cannot have human consciousness. We need you to prepare them to be the next Horsemen of the Apocalypse. We need you to wipe them clear of their humanity. Destroy their souls."

"Well, Mr. Hades, that is certainly a 'can-do,'" Brother Bainbridge replied. "I always say, 'Discipline is the continual process of teaching a child to learn self-discipline.'" The charmingly middle-aged man turned a cheeky wink and prolonged his words, "But we haven't discussed the subject of payment."

"I've already offered to aid in finding your totems," he reminded him.

Brother Bainbridge shook his head, "I'm not interested in merging Hell and Earth in the vision of the collective. If I am doing the work, I should not only have a seat at the table but head it."

"You would use the Horseman to overthrow your brothers?" the Hallowed One asked.

Brother Bainbridge nodded, "The Hundreds of Hells that exist are divided. Everyone is having their own little Apocalypse nowadays. I say, let's not forget where we came from, and unite under one rule. Mine. Do what you will with the Earth."

"Clear the Angels," the Hallowed One offered, "and you can have all the Hells you want."

"I believe he said all of them," Diamond barked and placed a hand on her shapely hip. She threw back a lock of her shiny black hair and rolled her hazel eyes. The woman was human, except for the high level of plastic installed through surgery. Every inch of her body was exaggerated, and she covered it with a skintight pink leather bodysuit. "I work for the supreme being over here, so I don't normally get involved in mouthy negotiations, but I will bring a cheese grater to your face if you try anything funny, Hades lord of the Dead or not."

"Threaten me, girl, and that ring will do little to protect you," Hades cautioned.

"Enough," Brother Bainbridge interrupted, "I will audit the angels."

She glanced toward Neil and seductively muttered, "How about we start with this one. I think he needs a little rest and relaxation…"

"I'm sure it would be a pleasure working with you." Brother Bainbridge replied in a robotic tone as he turned to the outspoken, scantily clad woman. "The mark of the Horsemen is on them," his voice was monotone yet optimistic. Brother Bainbridge dashed over to Neil and took hold of his chin. "I will clear them in no time. I don't think these kids are going to give me any trouble at all."

"Get the f—" Neil tried to speak but Brother Bainbridge grabbed both sides of his face with such vigor it allowed no space to move.

Feverishly he spat, "Are you unhappy with your life? Do you feel like you lack control or find yourself in situations where you feel utterly helpless? Does existence seem bland or unenjoyable?" Brother Bainbridge paused his sanctimonious words and reveled at Neil's detainment in a moment of pride. "Everything you know is a lie."

Swiftly, his perfect white teeth ripped off a small chunk of his wrist. As the short alien-like demons held Neil in place, Brother Bainbridge forced his bleeding wound into Neil's mouth. He grinned as he spoke, "I know how much it hurts, but your human spirit is weighing you down. We must remove it from your flesh. Luckily, I have just the thing. My blood is a cleansing detox. A tonic that will help you through this transition. Have a drink…."

"Drink!" the short men chanted. "Join us!"

Reactively, Neil wanted to throw up again, but the black ooze trickled down his throat, and suddenly he felt calmer. The demons forced him onto a massage table in the middle of his cell. The bright white light above blinded him and drained his power.

He was vulnerable, but he hadn't felt this safe since he became an angel. Neil's nostrils flexed as he continued to drink Brother Bainbridge's blood as if it was the only thing that could sate his hunger. Sweet and sugary, it tasted like Kool-Aid. After each gulp of the candied liquid, Neil could feel his fear and panic melt away.

All he could hear was Brother Bainbridge. "You were never an angel, my dear sweet boy." Brother Bainbridge's voice was like a mother's tender call in an empty world, "God has been dead for eons. Otherwise, he would have saved you by now. Open your mind, Michael, your father, has forgotten you. Let me into your mind."

"Never! I'm a psychic too, you son of a bitch," Neil spat and regurgitated bits of black liquid onto his hairless chest, then wrestled with his bind. "Where's Aurora? What have you done with her?"

"Please," Brother Bainbridge begged, then exhaled loudly but kept his polite persona. "Stay in a child's place. You will be reunited soon."

Light waves fanned the aching throb on Neil's temples. Like vines that grew toward the sun, his mind bloomed and expanded. Without vision, he could see the horrific depths of the volcanic dungeon disguised like a spa. He could taste the blood and smell the fresh pine deodorizer they coated the upper floors with.

Indivisible lines sprouted from his head like a web made of static. The strings flew out for miles, and Neil understood every inch of land as though he were standing right there. He could name the trees, describe the rocks, and detail the weather. It was an awareness he had never reached. While the mental lacework flourished, he began to notice human life. They floated around like huffs of stale dust, and when Neil's mind touched them, he understood them as well.

Each human he connected with was filled with tragic memories and past traumas. Neil counted: 1, 100, 600… gorged with pain, they screamed and fought, lied and murdered. Such tortured souls were better off dead.

Then… Aurora.

Chapter 3: Why Must I Follow Your Rules?

"As early as 1950 the CIA developed a UFO office to deal with the sightings of unidentified flying objects over Nevada. When people first saw the U-2 spy plane flying, no one knew what they were seeing. The CIA used that disinformation to their benefit by fostering an alien mythology."

Annie Jacobsen

The infant child's searing voice sliced through the air like a barrage of arrows, then bounced off the color-coded candles and the alphabetized books on the shelves. She had everything from *Accessories Amazing: Assorted Articles and Advice* to *Xanax Zoo*. Victoria Harvey's shoulder-length blonde hair was tightly wound in a bun, shoulder-length. Her flamboyant makeup blanketed most of the wrinkles in her forehead as she narrowed her brow and rocked her wailing son.

Her electric stare scrutinized the plump mocha-skinned detective that nervously perspired on her modern leather and iron couch. Fragrant cinnamon and oak scents rushed from a glass bowl of potpourri that sat on the wooden coffee table between the woman and the officer.

Paintings of British soldiers nested inexpensive frames, and the lemon peels' bitter taste coiled through the home. It was humid, and Martin's bald head reminded Victoria of a mahogany bowling ball.

Victoria had special dishware she used only when guests were over. They were expensive, and she was careful never to get any scratches or breaks in them. She placed her lemon squares on the table and sat across the man.

"Lemon Square," Victoria offered with a sarcastic tone. She released the long deep breath she held since he came through the door, "Officer...?"

Martin Hightower swallowed two of the small yellow cakes and wiped away the beads of moisture collected around his receding hairline. He realigned his thick navy blue tie and spoke in a deeply concerned voice, "Ms. Harvey, it is my understanding that you have reported the father of your son missing about two weeks ago?"

"It was three and a half weeks ago," Victoria corrected, then swayed Zachary in her arms and rolled her eyes. "Pathetic, almost a month now and still no results!"

"Ma'am," Martin sighed, "a lot's been going on in this city. Did you hear about the guy who robbed a liquor store, shot himself in the head nine times, and a python crawled from his skull? We're still trying to figure that one out…some sick sexual ritual we can concur. Over a hundred thousand people go missing every year…"

"And how many of them have you found? I'm not interested in your problems right now! We're in New York! We're too busy trying not to get sick with whatever is going around than worry about anyone else!" She continued as though she already knew his answer, "So if you haven't found him, why are you in my apartment, detective?" Victoria sneered as she shifted her crying child and raised an arched eyebrow. "He's not in my living room! Shouldn't you be out there searching for him right now? Maybe checking with that Blood Wolf gang? I've heard they've been causing trouble lately."

"That's exactly what I'm doing," the pudgy man leaned forward saying. "I believe his case may be connected to a few others. Before Neil disappeared, did you notice any strange behaviors such as paranoid delusions, prophetic speeches, suicidal thoughts, or threatening comments?"

Victoria's thin red lips flattened into a straight line as she fussed, "Are you insinuating that the father of my child is some kind of terrorist? I already told you I don't know why he was at that church! I don't know why it exploded; I've never been there in my life. Didn't they say it was a gas leak? These are all questions I would ask Neil myself if you would do your job!"

"On April 17th, the day of the explosion, my partner was thrown through the windshield of a police car and is still in a coma," Martin confessed; his fingers were as thick and greasy as the sausages he had for breakfast that morning. He placed a photograph of Rhion on the coffee table, then followed it with three other large pictures. "Your ex-boyfriend, along with Ezekiel Wallace, Aurora Haith, and Amanda Randall, all went missing that day. Do you know what Neil's relationship was with any of these people?"

"Neil doesn't have relationships," Victoria spat venomously. "Neil has a career!"

"Actually," Martin spoke coyly, licked his thumb, and rubbed out a jelly stain on his white t-shirt. "Neil has not been employed for a while, it turns out."

Victoria stood from her chair with such an unnerved, blind anger that Zachary almost slipped from her arms. In complete horror, the baby's cry penetrated the walls and stormed through the neighbors' apartments. Her eyes were like icebergs, lifeless, cold, and dangerous. In an even tone, her voice was as steady and powerful as a rushing river, "He...didn't tell me that. If he quit his job, then I know that something is wrong with him. He goes crazy when he's not working. How is he going to pay for college when Zachary gets into Yale?"

"I can't answer that question for you, ma'am," Martin confessed as he collected the photographs off the coffee table and buried them in his leather briefcase. "But I did make a promise to my partner. Your ex-boyfriend has a lot of secrets, and I will find them out."

"Well, keep me in the loop," Victoria instructed, then stomped to the front door and unhinged the gold chain that held it. "Thank you for the update, but I think we both have work to do."

Martin stuffed two lemon squares in his pocket, then exited the premises.

Neil's stomach coiled with pangs of hunger as he curled into a fetal position. Had the world ended? Had he failed? The heat in the sauna numbed his consciousness, and all he wanted to do was crumble. By this time, Neil was too weak to snap a twig. However, through his hysteria, a voice began to trickle through. It was a soft, familiar whimper.

Someone he knew was crying. Maybe he was more powerful than he thought. Unable to control the volume of the moaning, he followed it straight to the right wooden wall… then through it.

Aurora.

He placed his palms on the oak planks. Though he knew he was not powerful enough to break them, he felt Aurora there. In his mind, he heard her cry. He sensed her in the same way he consumed the minds of others that surrounded him. Though the incongruous spikes in his mind were painful, Neil closed his eyes and felt comfort in her sound. It meant she was alive, and he was not alone.

Weakly, he repeated her name.

His consciousness had split in two.

Physically, his body remained in his cell, but his mental power caused him to be in two places at once. As a shadow, he stood in Aurora's cell. It was a sauna, but a jail cell built precisely like his. He tasted the sulfur and felt the heat on his skin as if he were really there.

Aurora was manic. He felt her immobilizing fear, and with a chilly burst, it ran up his arms in goosebumps. He had so many questions, but before he could have a chance to answer them, Aurora turned from her fetal position.

"Neil!" her voice shouted loudly in her head.

Aurora crawled up into a corner of the sauna, where she most closely felt Neil's presence. Dehydrated, her eyes burned red with distress as she questioned, "I can hear you… A-are you really here?"

"I'm here, I-I think I'm in your mind," Neil managed to muster a response.

His energy rebounded off like walls and felt like an echo. Desire conquered his confusion, and he cuddled Aurora; his fingers ran through her long locks. Touch was a vibrant sensation felt through the nerve endings of the mind. Every fiber of her resonated within him. Neil had no idea how he got into the room, but as he looked up at her face, he could smell her salty skin and caress the warmth in her nether regions.

Naked and terrified, Aurora was raw and as winsome as ever. Just when Neil had thought she died, her glistening ebony flesh was a sweaty masterpiece hardly covered by her raven mane. Her chest grew more prominent with every hysteric breath she took, and her wide chocolate eyes never looked so enticing above her tiny black mole. Aurora was undeniably strong, but Neil had never seen such valor in a vulnerable position.

Her emotions melted off her, and he soaked them in like butter on bread. He felt her moisten and her muscles tighten. Desolate and petrified, he planted his lips onto her. Her skin jounced and released beads of perspiration into the hot air.

She could feel him. Hard and steadily, he rocked her. Aurora's fingers crept in-between her thighs. The angel was sure Neil was there and knew he would protect her. Aurora graciously directed his fingers through tangled hair; his grasp at her neck and his searing heartbeat pounded at her back.

Aurora got wetter.

His gorgeous angel was alive. His fear subsided and was replaced with impulse. Without asking questions, Neil yearned for her body and enlaced his fingers with hers. He drove himself into her. She tightened around him. Neil let it sit there for a moment. He was not in the room, but this experience was all too real. Aurora closed her eyes and leaned back as if he was physically behind her.

Neil pushed himself in so deeply that he was lost with only her cocoa butter scent to guide him through the sweet void. Again and again, he pressed their bodies closer together and realized with every increased stroke that this moment was genuine. He was consumed by her soft skin but also relieved that she survived her skirmish with the Horseman of War.

"You can't be real…" Aurora doubted. She breathed heavily and turned to him as he was still inside of her, "Are you in my mind? H-how are you doing this?"

He could hear her thoughts, and she could listen to his. Neil could not stop. His hands pressed at her thighs, and he kissed her neck. "I don't know, I just felt you here, and I-I wanted to talk to you so bad. Are you okay?"

"Are you fucking kidding me? Does it look like I'm okay?" Aurora asserted in anger.

For a moment, she wondered if she had finally gone mad. However, she trusted Neil and knew to never underestimate him. He was in her mind, and she was comforted. Quivered with irritation and exhaust, she ran her fingers through her curly hair, and in a fragile whisper, she cried, "Neil… I'm so pissed off… I don't know what we're going to do."

"This man," the angel supposed as he shook his head, "is a psychic. I can feel it. He's trying to do something to us." Neil was convinced, as he reported the information. He faded in and out as he spoke, "They're trying to get rid of our humanity… turn us into monsters."

"Are you really here?" Aurora asked and quirked an eyebrow. "I think that bright light is poison or something. My powers aren't working like they used to; how are yours?"

"I don't know," Neil announced. "That man… He's trying to mentally destroy us. But I'm going to break us out of here. I don't know if this is some kind of Hell…"

"No," Aurora frowned at the wooden benches and a coal pit that never stopped steaming. Sweat dripped from her chin; she clung to the wall where she felt Neil's essence the strongest and continued to bounce on his lap. "Neil, I haven't eaten. I never felt so weak, but I had a vision. Ezekiel and Amanda are still alive. I don't know what these demons' plans are, but we're all trapped here in these hot cells. In this room, our powers aren't working. But, we're not too far apart…. less than a few feet. Maybe if you can connect all of our minds, we can figure out how to escape…"

"It feels like I haven't seen you in so long. I think they can wait a few minutes more…" Not long after he spoke, the mighty angel shut his eyes, and the hot steam rose from the raging coals. His fingers spread and arched with anticipation.

Aurora's voice was like a splash of cool water. Neil's body throbbed, and his blood stiffened his appendages. Like an animal, instinct enveloped him. His heartbeat faster as Aurora pulsated.

Neil was a balloon of heightening pressure. Before he could pop, though, nausea washed over him. The sickness lasted for only a second before the body of his lover became soft and spongy. He pressed his fingers deep into her flesh, and like damp cardboard, she tore open.

Blood streamed to the ground like water from an overflowed sink. Abruptly, Neil tried to release the angel, but as maggots rushed from her body, a force prevented him from moving. Aurora decayed with every passing moment. She looked back in horror as Neil was covered in blood and pale larva.

"N-neil…" she tried to speak as blood ran from her eyes. Neil was trapped inside her.

His lower lip dropped, but before he could muster a word, Aurora was gone and replaced with a bent over and stripped Brother Bainbridge. In complete horror, Neil fell back as the plump older man gazed over his shoulder with a delightful and almost innocent grin. He blew a kiss.

Like a sudden storm, Bainbridge swept the angel from his stance and single-handedly pinned him to the upper right corner of his sauna. Bainbridge tightened his grip around Neil's neck and inched closer to his face as they levitated several feet above the ground.

Bees buzzed past his ears, and slowly, Bainbridge's appendages lengthened. With every second, he grew larger until his mass was six times the size of Neil's. He hissed as he spoke, "Now, now, now, what exactly do you think you're doing?"

Neil jerked around in his bind and spat the humming bees away from his face. Bainbridge's hot breath smelt like burnt meat. When the demon drew in closer, his eyes and teeth became yellow and more reptilian. "Did you really think you could try that, my child? I am the Highest Operating Psychic in the Western Hemisphere. You cannot pull one over on me… without me knowing. You cannot trick me…. without me allowing it. And you cannot fuck me over unless I bend down and enjoy it, little boy. Your psychic abilities are nothing when compared to mine."

"I…I-I'm not scared of you," Neil was completely powerless but forced himself to speak.

"Don't worry; we can change that. Let us begin." Brother Bainbridge snickered and

vanished as Neil dropped to the ground like a steaming frying pan to kitchen tile.

"Get back in here and fight me!" Neil's war cry bounced off the glass door of his prison.

Frustrated and exhausted, Neil turned but jumped when he found that Bainbridge was behind him. The demeanor of the middle-aged man was serene as he folded his hands neatly beneath his potbelly. Neil had no idea what type of demon Bainbridge was, but the man vibrated with a dry and ashen essence he had never felt.

Neil quivered under the fluorescent lights. Part of him almost did not expect Bainbridge to return so suddenly, but now that he was here…. Neil had to kill him.

The entire room vibrated with a wave of intensity. Neil built velocity but had to push forth through the weakening shine of the light bulbs above him. Sweat felt like tiny needles that poked a pincushion from the inside out. Translucent beams of mental energy assembled around the room in massive spider webs.

Bainbridge smirked as the energy in the room overloaded then popped in small crackles of electricity. With blackened eyes and purple wings made of static, Neil was lifted off the ground. He waved an arm at the smiling creature, but the telekinetic blast hardly wrinkled Bainbridge's red sweater.

"Are you done?"

Wrapped in a ripple of reality, Neil's arms were forced to his sides. Air grew thick and became too dense for the angel to move. He was trapped. The room melted around him. Neil knew Bainbridge was controlling it. Each wall sweat blood so profusely it started to flood the room.

Neil curved his lips in exasperation. He was helpless to combat Bainbridge's warp of physical and mental existence. His hands shook in fear as they, too, began to dissolve.

Slowly, Bainbridge walked to the exit. "This is the worst part of the job," he sighed as he opened the door, and the room continued to fill with red liquid. "Now, be a good boy. I'll be back later."

Neil fell into a pool of blood that grew deeper every second. His heart pounded so heavily in his chest he failed to realize his wings were gone, and his eyes had returned to normal. Neil landed a fist on the heavy glass that held him.

Soon, the angel found himself swimming in blood and soon after he found himself drowning in it. The suffocation was mystical as it continued, hours after he should have died. There was no thought but the animal instinct to crawl free and the never releasing choke of death.

When Neil awoke, the room was bare. Neil plopped to the ground like a sack full of red meat and struggled for air. His eyes were red with sadism. In his mind, he had been drowning for hours, and his body heaved.

Before Neil could catch his breath, however, the door crept open, and into the room slinked Diamond Love. Delicately her pin-straight obsidian mane floated behind her as she shut the door. She wore a tight and tiny red skirt above long fishnet stockings and tall black high heels. Her fake light-blue eyes were like needles to Neil's stomach.

"You're acting up again?" she asked, raised an eyebrow, and cracked her knuckles. "You're not going to be able to beat him, you know?"

"W-who are you?" Neil's brain still crackled with psionic energy when he questioned. As he beheld Diamond, a sudden wash of sadness buried him. There was more behind her bitter exterior. It was like no demon he has ever observed. In the depth of her sullen hidden heart was a spark of warmth, "Y-you're a human…"

Diamond's nose wrinkled, and her robust lips puckered. In a single stride, Diamond struck Neil across his chin and knocked him out cold.

Chapter 4: What Have You Done to Me?

"I saw a wheel on the earth beside the living creatures, one
for each of the four of
them. As for the appearance of the wheels and their
construction: their appearance was like the gleaming of beryl.
[…] And when the living creatures went, the wheels went
beside them; and when the living creatures rose from the
earth, the wheels rose."
Ezekiel 1:15

"'Thy kingdom come, thy will be done on earth as it
is in Heaven…'" Tears rolled from Amanda's large eyes and
painted her supple rosy cheeks as she prayed. Her hair was a
blonde nest of knots, and her naked knees trembled on the
hardwood floor. At this point, Amanda was familiar with
terror, but this was a new depth she never thought she'd
reach. Her powers were greatly diminished, and alone,
Amanda had nothing to rely on but her prayers.

As she prayed, Amanda was hit squarely across the
jaw. She screamed out in shock but was pinned up against the
wall in her jail cell. Diamond Love had entered unnoticed.

The woman kissed her silver ring and tightened her grip around Amanda's throat.

"Good morning! How are we doing?" Brother Bainbridge announced and floated in like a spirit surrounded by bumblebees. Two of the gray shorter demons were by his sides. Diamond spit on the ground like an angry stripper, and Amanda struggled to cover her naked body.

"Bad," confused Amanda answered the question as honestly as possible. She scooped her breasts and crossed her legs, then crouched into a corner to cover herself. Confused, she didn't know what to make of Brother Bainbridge, "W-why are you asking? Is it because you really care, or are you just trying to be evil?"

"Oh, my poor sweet child, I do care." Brother Bainbridge exhaled woefully. "I love you. I love you so much I want to peel off your skin, strip by strip, and feed it to you."

"What?!" Amanda gasped in total horror. "You're joking! You wouldn't do that... You seem so nice."

Bainbridge and Diamond locked eyes for a moment before they erupted in a fit of laughter.

"You don't have to do…" Amanda swallowed a rock in her throat, "whatever it is that you're planning on doing! It's not too late! If you let me go, I can tell everyone you made a mistake and that you're not such bad guys!"

Bainbridge continued, "That blood tonic that I gave you earlier can rumble your tummy. It begins the process to rid your body of all the nasty little human toxins you may have in your vessel. You see, most angels create a vessel to walk on this dimension; you were born with one, so you are bound to it. In extension, your body traps your soul and links it to the earth, like no angel ever created. You have wild power; however, you are bound by my limitations. But my detox will take care of that, it's good for you, trust me, I made it myself."

It was true. Amanda had tried to spit out the demon's blood, but the candied ooze coated her tongue and like an iced tea; it was a refreshing burst of happiness in a hellish dungeon. She had to admit that she enjoyed drinking the Kool-Aid. It was as instinctual as an infant's longing for his mother's milk.

The sweater-wearing demon nodded toward Diamond. She flipped her long straight black hair and snatched Amanda up by the back of the neck as effortlessly as she would a rag doll. With a loud thud, she slammed Amanda face down into the massage table and strapped her in so that her all the angel could see was their feet through the headrest.

Chapter 5: Fire Ring I: Recognition of the Unmanageable

> "See what kind of love the Father has given to us, that we should be called children of God; and so we are. The reason why the world does not know us is that it did not know him. Beloved, we are God's children now, and what we will be has not yet appeared; but we know that when he appears we shall be like him, because we shall see him as he is."
> **John 3:1-2**

"Thank you for joining our exclusive little club! You see, the Volcano Room is a special little place at Obelisk House enjoyed only by our most exclusive members," Bainbridge announced and smiled down to Amanda. "Here in the Volcano Room, we specialize in full mind, body, and soul reconstruction. We aim to open the doors to a fresh beginning. When you leave here, you will feel renewed and refreshed. A totally new person. Those pesky angelic souls will be lifted, and you will achieve your full potential." Brother Bainbridge continued as Amanda wiggled in her binds.

Tears created a small puddle under her face, but it dried quickly under the heat. Two smaller gray demons pulled over a tray of lit candles and burning fragrances. A blinding white light covered her sight, and suddenly, she was trapped in her memories.

16 Years Ago

"'Dearly beloved, we are gathered together to join this man and woman in Holy Matrimony." The deep voice of Father Guilherme always sent shivers down Amanda's spine, but today, she could hardly contain her glee.

Howard and Becky Randall joined hands as the holy man continued his sermon. Amanda was in a baby blue bridesmaid gown that she and her mother picked together. This was Becky's second wedding to her first husband, and Amanda had never felt so honored to be around to see her mother and father relive their storybook wedding after twenty-five years. She squealed with excitement but was guilty that she almost felt even more involved in this wedding than her mother was.

Every decision was filtered through Amanda; it was her dream wedding. With each flower, she could tell the story of how she and her mother laughed, how they argued over centerpieces and how she accidentally spilled Kool-Aid over the tailored napkins.

Her parent's perfect marriage was the only constant in her life. Their love served as a pillar of strength for the blonde teen. They never argued or raised their voices. Her mother treated her father as a king and never complained.

"'Unto the woman,' Father Guilhreme spoke, 'I will greatly increase thy sorrow and thy conceptions. In sorrow shalt thou bring forth children, and thy desire shall be subject to thine husband, and he shall rule over thee.'" The bald priest fixed his robes as he spoke to the beaming couple.

Amanda bit her jealous lower lip as he finished reciting scriptures. She couldn't help it. This was her mother's second wedding, and she hadn't even kissed a boy yet. The teen let out a sad sigh as she forced on a smile and cheered at the part she had been waiting for.

"Wilt thou have this woman to be they wedded wife?"

Chapter 6: Fire Ring 2: Hope and Rehabilitation

"And God blessed them. And God said to them, "Be fruitful and multiply and fill the earth and subdue it and have dominion over the fish of the sea and over the birds of the heavens and over every living thing that moves on the earth."
Genesis 1:28

The sweet, sugary blood of Brother Bainbridge leaked over Neil's puckered lips. Powerless, he was chained to the massage table. He took long, heavy gulps of air and wiggled his fingers, just to remind himself they were still attached. Neil had no idea how long he had been in the Volcano Room, but his body could not adapt to the hours of torturous heat and poisonous gases.

The two Z'New moved like overweight gray penguins as they lugged over a tray of red and gold candles. A bowl of incense burned in the center of the tray, and the smell of rotten eggs filled the room. The black diamond-eyed creatures placed the burning assortment directly under Neil's nose.

"My blood will cleanse your insides, but it only makes you ready for your first treatment. Here at the Volcano Room, we like to begin the audit with a little aromatherapy. Just relax, my friend. To become clear, you must give up everything you know. Show me what is inside your soul,"

The angel's eyes rolled into the back of his head, and within moments he was asleep.

20 Years Ago

Neil slammed his locker as loudly as he could. This was always a contest among the pre-teen boys at Jamie Morales Elementary. With the blush, he had caught the attention of the slightly older Victoria Harvey. She was a bit taller and the first to develop curves in her class. Victoria had long blonde curls that stopped right above her buttocks. Her mother let her color her hair with pink streaks and wear blue eyeshadow around her bright green orbs. Victoria was easily the prettiest girl in school, and everyone knew it.

She gently closed her locker and winked over her shoulder. With perfect dimples, she flashed an ideal grin then shuffled down the hallway. Neil blushed as Derrick and Christopher congratulated him with high fives and hoots.

"Dude, she totally likes you!" Derrick's voice cracked as he cheered.

"Shut up," Neil warned and bashfully punched his friend in the shoulder. "I don't even know if she knows me yet!"

"My older brother is in her class, and he said that she 'goes all the way,'" Christopher jiggled his eyebrows while he joked. "Like under your underwear and stuff."

"You should invite her over!" Derrick gasped with excitement. "She'd probably let you touch her boob!"

"Are you kidding me?" Neil folded his arms and asked in disbelief. "My Mom is always home! Except for when she goes to church, but they always take me with them."

"So, just pretend you're sick!" Christopher offered. He was always the smart one. Readily he continued, "They'll let you stay home if you get sick!"

Neil's face winced in deep thought, "Doesn't Jimmy have chicken pox?"

Chapter 7: Fire Ring 3: Contacting A Higher Power

"Then God said, "Let us make man in our image, after our Likeness. And let them have dominion over the fish of the sea and over the birds of the heavens and over the livestock and over all the earth and over every creeping thing that creeps on the earth."
Genesis 1:26

Aurora's long raven ringlets were caked with the sappy red slime that seeped from Brother Bainbridge's wrist. She was strapped to the massage table, and right away, Aurora fell slave to the toxic liquid. Her mind clouded, and her vision blurred. She felt dizzy, yet a sense of euphoria eased her tense muscles and numbed her mind.

The skinless demons, Z'New, placed the tray of red and gold candles underneath her nose; she was in a trance. Intense warmth floated off this platter and was unbearably potent. Lit candles surrounded a bowl of boiling viscera and smelt like defecation. Bainbridge was giving them all six-year-old what is this?sc; Ezekiel was trying to invade their minds. She wrinkled her nose at first but then breathed deeply as she fell unconscious.

23 Years Ago

"But Mom!" Aurora shouted and fisted her six-year-old fingers and shouted at the top of her lungs. The schedule forced upon her caused her to work more hours than an adult family. She had no control over what she did because her mother managed every hour of her life.

Exhaustion irritated her, and her hormonal rage only added to her constant outbursts. Stubborn tears clung to the edges of her large brown eyes. The entire week she had spent hours preparing for this audition. Since she was finally at a weight, her mother approved, and it was one of the many tryouts her mother had lined up for her. Aurora gripped the edges of her frilly yellow dress. This was her first real audition, and the chaos backstage increased her fright.

Aurora hated these overwhelming showcases, but she could tell they were really important to Rebecca. Makeup artists scurried, stage mothers stressed, and the Miss Pre-Pre-Teen USA workers dashed about like headless birds. As far as Aurora was concerned, she didn't fit in with the other children. They were mean, rich, white, and soulless; Aurora was just a meek dark-skinned girl with a slightly underdeveloped body.

"I want to play soccer!" Aurora objected. She watched as the other stage mothers practiced scales and dance routines with their daughters. The competition was thick, and she had never been so intimidated in her life.

"Children are to be seen and not heard!" Rebecca Haith instructed while blanketing her child's face with powder, and she snarled. Aurora coughed a bit, and Rebecca scoffed in annoyance, "And don't you want to do pretty things? You'll never have a career in soccer. Trust me; these pageants will be the beginning of an amazing career for you!" Roughly, she fixed Aurora's dress as she spoke, "Now you're the only black girl, so you're going to have to work twice as hard. Like it or not, you're going to stick out. Stop crying, or you'll ruin your makeup."

"Mom," she begged. Aurora puckered her lower lip, and her eyes welled. "Karen and I said we were going to join the soccer team together; she's my best friend!"

Rebecca exhaled loudly and retrieved a hairbrush from her purse. She pulled Aurora close to her and was not gentle with a single stroke as she brushed her daughter's mane. Her mother sighed when she spoke, "You really need to find new friends, Aurora. It's not that I don't like Karen… however, I'm sorry, but she is a troglodyte."

Aurora closed her eyes and struggled to speak as her head was yanked in every direction. "W-what's a troglodyte?"

Rebecca almost growled but, without hesitation, spat, "Karen is a troglodyte. Karen is a frumpy hog of a disgusting girl. She weighs too much for a girl her age! All that weight is disturbing to look at. It makes everyone around her uncomfortable. Her parents really should do something, but she does come from a poor, disgraceful family after all. I don't want anyone to associate you with those qualities. Her mother is big too. All they do is sit around and eat and watch movies and absorb taxpayer's money. You can't get lazy. You need friends that can take you places, not a rambling oaf who plays in the mud."

"Opening act!" a man with a skinny tie yelled.

All twelve girls were forced into line by their overbearing mothers. Aurora threw up her hands, but Rebecca batted her into the roundup with a single swipe. Aurora's heart was in her stomach. She wrapped her fingers around her warm belly as the opening music began, and mothers cheered on their children with final words of encouragement.

"Remember to keep your head up Aurora," Rebecca was as stern and lifeless as a brick with her words.

Aurora pointed her chin up and smiled just as she was taught. As the line began to move, her body trembled. She stepped foot onto the stage. The first row of the audience was filled with a panel of judges, and the back rows were cluttered with friends and family of the contestants.

During the opening act, the girls marched to the end of the stage, curtsied, then pranced back. Her lungs filled with air. How could her mother say that about her best friend? Was she right? Tears fought their way out of her like water out of a popped balloon.

Her eyes were wide and wet. As the music played, she walked, but with every step, cried a little less.

Chapter 8: Fire Ring 4: Identifying Faults

"For we are strangers before you and sojourners, as all our
fathers were. Our days on the earth are like a shadow, and
there is no abide"
Chronicles 29:15

Though Brother Bainbridge successfully audited three
angels, he still had blood left for another. Ezekiel was the
final prisoner in the line. As the other three angels cried in
their sleep, Brother Bainbridge stammered over to Ezekiel.
His heart was in his throat, and he was hyperventilating.
However, at this point in his life, fear was an emotion he used
to.

"Y-you won't be able to control us, you know,"
Ezekiel warned. "Not forever. I-I will k-kill you when I get
out of here."

Brother Bainbridge adjusted his red sweater and
coughed slightly, "When you get out of here, you will be
clear. All this rage that sloughs off you will be erased."

"No!" Ezekiel urged as the Z'New demons placed the
fragrant assortment of candles and blood below his face.

"Come now; it's for your own good. Breathe it all in," Brother Bainbridge advised with a smirk. "Join us."

18 Years Ago

Walking home from school was his favorite time of day. It was the only time Ezekiel had his mother all to himself. He beamed with excitement because this third-grader had a very busy lunch hour. Over the blares of cars, he dished the gossip. Petra revealed she had a crush on Xavion; Whitney and Leah were no longer friends; his gym teacher had passed gas in front of the entire class; and most importantly, his art teacher said that his drawings were the best she had ever seen.

"I made these for you! Mrs. Penelope said we could draw whatever we want!" Ezekiel squealed, then squeezed his mother's hand and held his finger paintings in the other. Most children in Ezekiel's class hated open-ended art projects, but he cherished the challenge. Ideas popped in and out of his head fluently, and when he got them onto paper, there was no greater satisfaction. With knowledge of his mother's love of birds, Ezekiel crafted three pieces of work that focused on her favorite animal: the dove.

Unlike most students, Ezekiel took extreme pride and esteem in his art. As the only child of a complicated family, he often questioned his worthiness but never knew how much his mother cared for him. He explained, "It's a picture of a dove flying over a rainbow! Some birds like to fly over things; they can even fly over a rainbow."

"That's nice, Ezekiel," Lauren sighed at the garrulous child and longingly stood before their apartment door.

4E was a cluttered home. Every inch of the Brooklyn apartment was covered with an item that triggered a memory. Lauren displayed every shell she found on every beach, empty liquor bottles from every spring break, and even old outfits that no longer fit. Even though Ezekiel knew that he would never understand every memory, he loved every object in his home that held history.

Once the door was opened, Ezekiel bolted toward the cabinet and fished out the tape. With a yell, the child dashed to the already cluttered refrigerator and proudly hung his newest paintings. His mother greeted her husband with a kiss but pulled away quickly. He already tasted like whiskey.

"Next, I'm going to take a picture of a phoenix!" Ezekiel announced and latched on to his mother's leg. "Do you know what a phoenix is? It's a magic bird!"

"Magical bird?!" Fred objected. He looked down at his son through chestnut downcast eyes, then swirled the ice around the half-empty Collins glass before he asked, "Did you take gym today?"

"I didn't feel well!" Ezekiel whined and attached himself to his mother's leg.

"You felt well enough to draw those faggotty pictures. Magic birds? Really? Ain't you got girls in your class? Shouldn't you be chasing after them?" Fred questioned, then shook his head in utter disgust. "Come."

Ezekiel's grasp on his mother's thigh grew tighter. He never really understood drinking; all he knew was that it made his father a different, scarier person. Fred stood up and grabbed Ezekiel by the collar. The balding man forced his son into the plastic chair in the kitchen. His father yelled, "Is that it? You queer or whatever you call it?"

Present Day

Diamond Love tightened the straps on Ezekiel's massage table. She ran a hand through her long, pin-straight black hair and licked her plump red lips. Brother Bainbridge stepped away from Ezekiel's hallucinating body and covered his open wound with his red sweater. As always, he had a genial grin, and he stepped toward the exit. Proudly he boasted, "Well, I think I've earned myself a nap."

"Not so fast, old man," Diamond said, rolled her ice-blue contact-covered eyes, and slammed Ezekiel's cell door closed. "Just how long do you think this is going to take?"

"Ms. Love, I'm learning everything about them. Their secrets, their pain, their essence will all be mine," Brother Bainbridge explained. "Once I truly know what horrors are buried in their souls, their humanity will fizzle. After all, we are a product of our experiences."

"Yeah," Diamond supposed before she placed a hand on her tantalizing hip. "But… how long is this going to take? A sexy ass bitch like me… this is not how I want to spend my Saturday nights. I thought you were the great Beelzebub.

Some…what is it? Like the H.O.P.? High Operating Psychic, or something? What's the hold-up?"

"Destroying a soul takes time, especially ones this powerful," Brother Bainbridge spoke as he turned to her. His long mouth thinned out like a pencil, and his wrinkles dropped as his permanent smile faded, "Stay in a child's place, Ms. Love. I've lived millennia before you were a thought in your parent's head. I know what I'm doing. They have a few more treatments to go. That's all. Have patience."

"And if I don't," she threatened as she cracked her knuckles around her silver ring.

Brother Bainbridge laughed a bit, "You mean your ring? The Seal of Solomon can't control everyone you meet; mind your manners."

"Yeah?" Diamond asked as she folded her arms. "If you thought so, you wouldn't have hired me to watch your back… and your front."

"It's important to feel special. But we both know that no matter how many scams you pull or jobs you take, you will always be nothing but pure white trash. You're a dirty little whore and always have been," Brother Bainbridge confessed and shrugged as he left the room. "Don't

overstep."

Chapter 9: How Do I Affect You?

Neil had no idea how much time had passed since he was asleep. He just knew that he refused to back down, even if Bainbridge was a more powerful psychic than he. Will and hope fueled his concentration. Like drops of ink in water, Neil's eyes filled with black, and his mind opened up invisible connections that strung him and the rest of the angels together.

Along with Aurora's mind, he shuffled in Ezekiel. He could see them clearly as if he were right in the room. He needed to act quickly before Bainbridge interrupted again. Aurora was right; Ezekiel was only a few feet away. Neil recognized his immutable anxiety and pain. The boy was lonely and tasted like a mouthful of saltless crackers, empty and dehydrated.

Neil gritted his teeth as though he had yips. Connecting their consciousnesses was like pulling at cold rubber, but finally, he could hear her. Amanda was terrified, defeated, and confused. She pulled at her long blonde hair and scratched her scalp until she bled.

"C-can everyone hear me?" Neil psychically questioned. It was almost as if he were in four places at once.

"Neil?" Ezekiel gasped in desperation as he clawed at his arms as though he still had sleeves. "You're alive?"

"We all are," Aurora could hear them both as clearly as well. She shuddered with the fear of Bainbridge's previous interception and asked, "Neil, are you sure this is safe…. what if…"

"We just have to talk quickly," Neil instructed and tussled with deliberation. "I know I can block him for a little bit, at least. He surprised me before. Never again."

"So… it was real…" Aurora wistfully murmured.

"Thank God!" Amanda's eyes lit up with childish delight as she cheered.

Her jaw dropped, and she took a breath full of the burning brimstone. A blinding light from outside of the sauna attacked her eyes, and when her vision returned, she could almost hear the boiling lava several miles below her.

Like the others, Amanda was trapped in the haunted sauna without a stitch of clothing. Embarrassed, she went to cover herself, but she was still exposed and vulnerable. Amanda summoned the strength for a scream but realized that they were connected through their minds.

"W-why are we naked?" Amanda crossed her legs and sunk in her elbows to hide her nudity as she asked. "W-where are we?"

"Hell," Neil responded.

"This is not Hell," Ezekiel interjected through tears. "I've seen Hell. This is some sort of holding prison."

"When have you seen Hell?" Neil asked.

"It's the ghetto version of Hell," Aurora confirmed, "half the price but twice the smells."

"Okay, so that means," Amanda muttered as she tried to process the situation. She looked around frantically and thought out loud, "Wait… can somebody tell me what that means?"

Neil fisted his hands in frustration. There was no time for silly questions. He started, "We have to get out of here. Formulate a plan. Everybody, except for Amanda, think…"

"That symbol," Ezekiel noticed and pointed to the intersecting triangles that were connected by a curved line. "I've seen that symbol before. It's the sign of an ancient religion… An old cult. They believed in cleansing the human soul through tortuous procedures. I thought they died out a long time ago…"

"We're at the Obelisk House," Neil referred to the sign and logo he had seen earlier.

"That hospital, spa place?" Aurora asked. "I've heard about this place… It's in downtown. That place is supposed to be a five-star resort. Not covered in blood."

"It was built over cursed grounds," Ezekiel revealed. "Don't ask me how but I-I can sense the echoes of death… I-I think this is some sort of underground, demonic chamber…"

"It sounds like we should probably just leave…." Amanda announced, then squinted wiggled her fingers at the glass door that trapped her in the steaming prison. However, the glass and wood remained unchanged. Her powers were stifled. She confessed, "But, I can't even change shape."

"Remain calm," Neil ordered and held his temples in his hands. "I can sense your panic…"

Ezekiel studied the symbols on the wall and read out loud, "I can't read all of these… but there's an ankh…"

"What's an ankh?" Aurora questioned.

"The one that looks like a cross with a circle on top. It's an Egyptian symbol, I think,"

Ezekiel hypothesized, "It means 'human' and 'life.'"

"Except there doesn't seem to be anything human here…" she scoffed. "Look at the bright side," Amanda muttered through sniffles, "it could have meant 'monsters' and 'death.'"

"This is the best part of the job," Martin mumbled as he grabbed a handful of sugar cookies from the large plastic tray then drank unsweetened iced tea from a plastic cup that rested on a paper doily. The small apartment had the faint scent of lavender air fresheners. Though three fans blew at

him from different directions, it was so hot Martin's plaid
button-up shirt was wet in the center and around his armpits.

"Did you say you wanted pigs in a blanket or a Hot
Pocket?" Sylvia Goldenblatt offered with a twinkle as her
fists disappeared into her hips. With a face full of crumbs,
Martin fell blank in a moment of careful consideration.
Sylvia beamed at him through poorly applied red lipstick and
rushed off as she asserted, "Don't worry, I'll make you a little
of both! I insist! No one leaves my house hungry!"

The plump gray-haired woman quickly headed
toward the kitchen in her jelly slippers. There she found her
carrot-topped son; he sat on the blue kitchen counter and
chewed on an apple. Sylvia slapped his knee before she made
her way to the refrigerator and scolded, "What did I tell you
about sitting there? You'll fall off and hurt yourself!"

She tore open the freezer door and pulled out the
frozen packages of food while she complained, "I swear, he
doesn't stop eating! It's getting ridiculous!"

"Really, Mom?" Cody replied before he jumped off
the countertop in protest. "Not my Hot Pockets?"

"Well, he just keeps eating!" Sylvia admitted. She threw up her arms and tossed the icy dishes into the oven, "What do you want me to do?"

"Let's just see what he wants before he eats us out of the house and home," Cody suggested, then flung his apple core into the trash and walked into the living room with his mother close behind him.

"As if you pay for anything!" Sylvia shouted. "At least he makes a decent salary!"

The two entered the room while Martin licked the sugar off his fingers as he stared wide-eyed at the television as the reporter spoke loudly.

"I stand here at Pop's Diner where witnesses claim: hundreds of bloodthirsty rats literally rained from the ceiling and brutally attacked this small restaurant's regular guests," Jackie Adams announced as she held the microphone closer to her lips. "Leaving seventeen seriously injured and taking the life of two, Eric Nelson and his wife, Barbara. The owner of this establishment, Tollar Keith, claims to have never had a problem with vermin and suggests foul play. But the facts exist, and the questions remain: Where did the mice come from, and what drove them to murder? Police are on the scene to investigate how the rodents got into the ceiling and why they had such an intense craving for human blo—"

Sylvia turned off the television and snuggled into her noisy plastic-covered armchair while Cody settled beside her on the edge of the seat. Crumbles from Martin's mustache fell as he began, "Thank you for your time Ms. Goldenblatt; I won't take up too much of it. I just have a few questions about your neighbor, Neil Qin."

"Hasn't he moved out?" Sylvia's eyes tapered behind her green glasses as she celebrated, "Thank goodness! The floor hasn't been quiet since he started living the lifestyle'"

"He never notified his landlord of any relocation." Martin cleared his throat and asked, "Do you know where he went?"

"Why?" The freckled man in the cartoon spaceship sweater wiped his glasses clean, looked at the policeman, then asked, "Is he missing?"

"He was a partyer," Sylvia waved her finger and confessed, "and he kept bad company. Rude girls would come over at all times of the night and make noise! All that banging and screaming and arguing! Now I don't judge, but one time I even once saw a man visit for one of his loud parties; we don't need that in our neighborhood."

"Mother," Cody protested, "stop insinuating!"

"They would come over all times of night and bang things around," the older woman nodded as she spoke, "and they would scream and curse and sometimes leave with cuts and bruises! What do you call that?"

Martin wiped the perspiration off his shiny bald spot, and it dripped onto his yellow notepad before he asked, "Ma'am, are you saying he is a swinger?"

"What else could he be?!" Sylvia shouted. "If only you heard the way they would go at it, you'd swear they were fighting for their lives!"

"The honest truth is," Cody revealed, "he was our neighbor, but we hardly knew him. He kept to himself. Occasionally, loud noises did come from his apartment, but they could have been anything. Do you have any other questions, Detective?"

The massive man paused for a beat. He looked at his watch, then put away his notepad and settled back into the plastic-covered couch before he rubbed his stomach and reminded her, "Um, I was promised Hot Pockets…"

"Shhhhh," Mrs. Kapoor hushed her chatty kindergarten class as she sketched a large triangle on the chalkboard. In the thirty years she taught, she found this group of children the most active yet well-behaved. Mrs. Kapoor hardly needed her teacher's aide but was happy to have the young woman's company, especially in her older age.

Clara Rodriguez led the adolescents to their seats as they scrambled in from recess. This was just another part-time job for the indifferent nineteen-year-old brunette as she never had a fondness for children or their parents. She could have dealt without the messes, the notes written in crayon, or the repetitive silly songs.

Clara did, however, enjoy the simplicity of the innocents and the fact that they listened to her every word. The job could have been worse. Clara pointed a finger and a dirty look at one of the students as he reached in his knapsack for a bag of salted potato chips. She cautioned, "Don't let me see you open that bag! Pay attention!"

"Daniel!" Mrs. Kapoor scolded as she turned back to the board. "Use your fingers, class. How many sides does a triangle have?"

Slowly, Daniel popped open the blue bag. Clara stood from her chair and raised her eyebrow, and cautioned stronger this time, "Not today, little boy, don't you play with me! I will take away a sticker, then you gonna be mad!"

Daniel shoveled the snack into his mouth as Clara snatched what was left from his fingers. She scowled down at the child, but before she could discipline him, a steady growl rumbled through the air.

Clara staggered rearward. One by one, the children stood from their seats. In unison, their eyes fell deadpan, and their lips vibrated with low guttural resonance. Each student had their eyes fixated on Clara. Goosebumps ran up her arms, and her heartbeat quickened. As they inched closer, she slowly retreated until she propped herself on the desk.

"What is going on, class?" Mrs. Kapoor raised her voice and stepped in front of her teacher's aide. The older woman showed no fear; Mrs. Kapoor clapped her hands loudly and instructed, "Everyone back to your seats!"

With the single-minded coordination of a school of piranha, the children bombarded Mrs. Kapoor. The tiny youngsters quickly took down the elderly teacher. In complete horror, Clara shrieked as blood stained the walls. She could hear the juveniles' small teeth crunch Mrs. Kapoor's bones as they tore flesh and muscle from her body.

"Ay Dios Mio!" she cried. Hot tears ran down the aide's face. Clara screeched then dashed toward the door. Once she escaped the classroom, she shut it behind her and wailed through the empty hallway as the children devoured her employer and friend.

Chapter 10: What Does It Matter?

"When a stranger sojourns with you in your land, you shall not do him wrong. You shall treat the stranger who sojourns with you as the native among you, and you shall love him as yourself, for you were strangers in the land of Egypt: I am the Lord your God."
Leviticus 19:33-34

"And did you know the deceased?" Jackie Adams coldly questioned. She wrinkled her thin nose and placed false pity behind her eyes as she shoved the microphone into Dr. Devanne Kapoor's face. She was slightly jealous of the young woman's beauty but wanted to appear sensitive to her loss. Jackie cleared her throat, then perched her pink lips and continued her line of questions, "Were you two… related?"

Devanne sat on the schoolyard bench. Time seemed to move slowly. She was utterly mortified. An emergency of this magnitude turned the elementary school into a frenzy. The yard was overrun with paparazzi and heart-rendered parents. Everything was a haze. Her chocolate glance was glazed over and as immense as a doe. Devanne had to remind herself to breathe. The young doctor could not look anywhere; instead, she focused on an imaginary red dot on the camera that kept her numb, "She… she was my sister."

"What type of relationship did your sister have with her students?" Jackie inquired as heartlessly as she would boil pasta.

"Ms. Adams," Devanne spat and jolted into reality, "I don't know if you're insinuating any actions taken by my sister would justify her being eaten alive by her entire kindergarten class, but if you are prepared to hear from our family attorney…and quite possibly… the back of my hand!"

"Oh no," Jackie cleared her throat as she focused her glimpse on the hot white light above the camera. "This is a tragic story. I was only wondering what, if anything, could merit such a fate?"

"I'm unsure…" Devanne murmured. "But I am beginning to wonder if there are other forces at work here…" She wiped the tears that leaked from her eyes and continued, "I am not a religious person and also not an apostate. I believe in science. But, this is something very demonic. Children don't… c-children don't do this. What is going on?"

"Welcome, to Modern Monsters: Men, Myths, and Mindlessness," an awkward man introduced, then scratched the irritated, red razor bumps on his freshly shaved neck and adjusted his tightly tucked in blue and orange checkered shirt. "I'm Marshall!" the twenty-nine-year-old screeched through a mouth full of braces then slicked a greasy sliver of oily black hair behind his ear.

"And I'm Willie!" his short and plump co-star's voice broke as he spoke boldly into his microphone.

The two uncomfortable Internet correspondents were the total embodiment of a nerd. True to stereotype, they both wore tight outdated clothes and large thick glasses. They smiled as they posed back to back in front of the unsteady camera Cody Golenblatt struggled with. The three reported from the middle of the schoolyard where they had run into Clara Rodriguez, the teacher's aide. Since the event had drawn so much mysterious publicity, Cody thought it would be a perfect idea to sneak in to film an episode of their web series. Modern Monsters: Men, Myths, and Mindlessness was on a low-quality MeTube Channel that received nearly twelve views a month. Still, Cody shared a passion with his lifelong friends to investigate the supernatural and otherworldly.

As Cody filmed, Marshall pointed around a small yellow device. He scanned the parking lot then the air around Clara as she stood in front of a large cement staircase. With the tiny gun-shaped machine, Marshall grinned as it beeped when he reached the windows. He supposed, "I can't believe the Infrerted Thing picked up these radiation readings!"

"Cut!" Cody declared, then lowered the camera and corrected Marshall, "It's called an 'Infrared Thermometer,' and if you don't know how to read it, you should just let me do it!"

"We've been through this a hundred and fifteen times!" Marshall stomped and announced. "You can't be on camera! Girls like my braces; I look terrific next to Willie, and you're the best with gadgets, so you operate the camera! Can you please try to be mature about the situation?"

"This is supposed to be our show!" Cody objected. "I know the machines, and I find the leads! I want some camera time!"

As the infrared thermometer silenced, Clara backed away slowly and began to retreat before Willie caught her arm and pleaded, "I'm sorry! We're not usually like this!"

"What news station did you guys say you were from again?" Clara asked suspiciously and lifted an eyebrow.

"Don't worry about it," Marshall snapped and gestured for Cody to raise the camera. He repositioned his glasses and closed in on Clara like a human scarf. "You said you were there and actually witnessed the kindergartners devouring their beloved teacher?"

"Yes, I was!" Clara exclaimed and rolled her neck, "Let me tell you, it was so scary! They were so hungry, and I was like, 'Wait until lunchtime, my sweet little Bambinos,' and that is when the babies went crazy! They tried to eat me, and I was like 'Ay Dios Mio, what happened?' Then they ate Mrs. Kapoor like that. I have never seen anything like it."

Marshall leaned in closer and asked, "Can you comment on the level of possible demonic possession that might have been in the room?"

"What?" Clara asked and blinked.

Jackie Adams immediately took the position in front of Marshall. Her nostrils flared, and she placed a hand on her boney hip and began, and she declared, "Channel 9 News. Being that I don't see any press badges on you three, I believe we were next up for this interview. Where are you guys from?"

After the three were unable to come up with an answer, Jackie waved her hand in the air as though she was swatting away a fly and spat, "I thought so. Move along now…" She placed her hands on her hip and called to her cameraman, who was listening to his headphones, "Puck!"

Bobbing his head, the skinny man recited the rap,

"'The name's Anansi, I got coin, and I fancy,

Pretty girls, short skirts, no panty,

Uh, and against all odds,

Fuck the Twilight of the Gods

Fear not, I'm the king of the block

Bitch, now suck my Ragnarok!'"

Angrily, she called him again and hissed at the redhead in glasses, "Why are you still here?"

In defeat, Cody lowered the camera and trotted away, "Curses, foiled again!"

Marshall fisted his hands in rage and followed Cody off the school parking lot, "Well, we lost it. If I let you be on camera for one shoot, will you promise never to interrupt again?!"

Cody happily nodded.

"Where are we going next?" Marshall asked as he walked out of the school parking lot, crushed.

"I figured we could check out some more Hot spots," the freckled redhead confirmed.

"Hot spots?"

"I call them Hot Spots. It's when supernatural energy is chained to geographical areas. Could be a haunting… or just trapped energy. Maybe a burial ground or sacred ruins." Cody packed the camera into the bag, "Like the Donald Wood Library… Solace… the park. I just have to scope one out."

"If that infer-whatever gun can get us some ratings, I'm down," Marshall squealed. "I want to see real spirits. If there really are spirits there, that would make for great t.v., and you know it!"

Every inch of the fallen angel ached with agony. Trapped in a sauna, sweat dripped from his brow and burned Neil's eyes. Drained, his attempts to struggle with the glass doors failed. He took a deep breath of the sulfur-filled air and looked toward the sky. The fumes made him high. Why did Brother Bainbridge keep him alive? He had no idea how long he had been in the Volcano Room, and his mind was too jumbled to come up with a plan. The only thing he could think of was the sweet taste of Brother Bainbridge's blood.

He scanned Aurora, Ezekiel, and Amanda as they sat in their heated cages and strapped to the massage tables. Dried tears were washed away by waves of sweat. Weak, tired, hungry, and noticeably on the brink of death, they felt each other through Neil's psychic touch.

"W-we will get through this," Neil managed to whimper as he connected their minds.

"Shut up," Aurora hissed. "We have to kill Brother Bainbridge. I'm going to rip his throat out with my teeth."

"If only we had our powers," Amanda pleaded. "We can't beat him without them."

"There is something in his blood," Ezekiel hypothesized. "He's doing something to us. What kind of demon is he?"

Amanda's long blonde hair was untamed, wet, and filled with grit. She spit strands of her mane from her mouth, "When I signed up to be a superhero, I didn't think this would happen."

"He must be keeping us here for something," Ezekiel deduced. "O-or, why keep us alive? We have to figure out what it is…"

Amanda's heart dropped into her stomach when she noticed Brother Bainbridge stood outside of her cell. His mouth was unnaturally large, and his grin could terrify a shark. His usual entourage surrounded him; Diamond Love, Z'New, the smaller skinless trolls with pumpkin-sized heads and black oval eyes, and of course, the busty nurses with gray reptilian faces. Amanda swallowed a rock in her throat, "He's here…"

Chapter 11: Fire Ring 5: Past and Present Wrong Doings

"Sometimes the same person would write multiple times hoping for a different answer. Many felt that the records were too benign and that the Government [must be] 'hiding' the real stuff. Often there were allegations of coverup of deliberately hiding or destroying the documents. The National Archives still gets a fair amount of inquiries relating to UFO's and folks have come in looking for other records in accessioned US Air Force records in particular. So, Roswell, Area 51, Majestic-12, Projects Mogul, Sign, Grudge, and Twinkle continue to fascinate and draw researchers to examine our holdings for aliens."

Richard Peuser

"You should know by now," Diamond sounded surprised. "Brother Bainbridge never misses an appointment, and he's very prompt. Who you talking to?"

"Oh…" Amanda winced. "You know me; sometimes, when I'm bored, I talk to myself. You shouldn't eavesdrop!" Amanda was sick to her stomach but urged on, "We weren't talking about you! Haven't you done enough already?"

"Good Morning, my friend," the man greeted, balanced his blue tie, and revealed a thick wand-like structure from his sweater. The top of the metal object blinked with a tiny red light, "Today is a very special day because today, your body must go through a special treatment I like to call the 'Fire Ring.'"

"I hope you're lubed up," Diamond whispered seductively into Amanda's ear before slapping the blonde with the silver ring. The angel was powerless, and Diamond was as strong as a bull. She lifted Amanda off the table with a single hand.

Amanda screamed. She knew that kowtowing to the demon was wrong; however, a bubbling thirst within her called to obey. She had to admit, a large part of her wanted the torment.

11 Years Ago

"That's why we must abstain from sex and all temptations," Amanda finished and nodded confidently to the students who sat in a circle around her. Proudly, Amanda ran the after-school program "Teens for Christ" for six months now. Encouraged by her mother, her group of five high school colleagues met twice a week in an open classroom to discuss current issues and what it meant to be a Christian in present times. Amanda started the club to add to her college resume but quickly treasured these meetings as a moment she could link up with like-minded people, exchange ideas and, of course, shine in front of a group.

This meeting's topic surrounded celibacy, and Amanda dominated the conversation as usual. It was imprinted in her at a very young age to abstain from sex until marriage, and she was overjoyed to teach her beliefs. Her immense smile showcased all of her white teeth like fine china in a glass case, and she instructed, "We must always hold ourselves to the one special person. Remember, God, the angels, even Grandma, could be watching. And that concludes our meeting. Thank you for coming, everyone!"

As the classroom emptied, Jason Sands sluggishly packed his book bag. Since Jason had joined the club, he had always kept to himself. He was tall, thin, and pale with long greasy black hair. As a rebel, he always wore tight, ripped jeans and a yellow bandana. Dirty and ransacked, it looked as though he hadn't showered in weeks and smelt as though he used onions as a deodorant. His reserved, shy demeanor concerned Amanda, but today he seemed to linger, even after being dismissed.

"Everything okay?" Amanda packed her Bible in her school bag and asked sweetly.

"You don't really believe all that stuff you were saying, do you?" Jason's voice was a bit raspy, but he played it off with his nonconformist-swag. "If anyone tells you they haven't had sex before marriage, they're either lying or pretty pathetic."

"That's not true," she was shocked and red in the face when she spoke. "My parents were virgins before they were married."

"Yeah, that's what they tell you," Jason sounded so sure as he pushed his long black tendrils behind his tiny pale ears. "You can't deny human urges. Not everything you see or hear is the truth."

"Some things are, though," Amanda confirmed with a nod. "There is magic in this world. I just saw a video online of an owl and a cat that were best friends! Can you believe that? It's true. You can't explain some of these things, Mr. Grump; you just have to believe them." Amanda placed a hand on his shoulder and admitted, "I've been worried about you…"

"Worried about me?" he gasped.

"Yes," Amanda continued. "You're always quiet, but now you're being rude for no reason. I think you might be Bi-Poland."

"Bipolar. You're the bipolar one if you really believe God even exists." Jason grumbled, raised an eyebrow, and strapped his bookbag around his back.

"Of course, he does!" Amanda's lips thinned into a line as she spoke and folded her arms defensively.

"Then why would he let all these bad things happen?" Jason spoke slowly and drew closer to Amanda. Gently, he removed a blonde strand of hair from her face and whispered. "And deny us the most intimate pleasures and human connections? What kind of god would create us with these urges…. then tell us we can't listen to them?"

With his every word, her heart pumped heavier. It was like her ribcage could explode at any moment. Confused and nervous, goosebumps ran across her arms when she finally found the strength to muster words, "W-why, are you here if you don't believe in God?"

"I guess I just think you're beautiful," he confessed. Jason leaned in and pressed his thin lips against Amanda's. She resisted at first but turned into putty as Jason wrapped his arms around her. "And I got some of those urges I want to share with you."

Jason kissed her neck, and panic rose within her. Her eyes darted toward the closed classroom door as she inched onto the teacher's desk. Amanda had never been kissed before, and the feeling excited her. It was almost like her lips were on fire, and an animal was unleashed in her body. Jason's hands unbuckled her jeans, and she became numb. Her mind knew it was wrong, but Jason was right: her body craved physical attention.

Chapter 12: Fire Ring 6: Letting Go

"For we do not wrestle against flesh and blood, but against the
rulers, against the authorities, against the cosmic powers over this
present darkness, against the spiritual forces of evil in the heavenly
places."

Ephesians 6:12

Brother Bainbridge seemed to float as he walked. He
was always so calm and controlled, and that is what terrified
Ezekiel the most. With tears in his eyes, Ezekiel bit his lower
lip. Anxiety imposed energy into his exhausted limbs.
Ezekiel shuddered and balled up in the corner the best he
could. The monster approached him, and Ezekiel muttered,
"W-what kind of demon are you?"

"We're friends," Brother Bainbridge lifted the silver
wand and laughed, "that's all you need to know. Ready for
your treatment?"

"I-is that some type of probe?"

Diamond tied Ezekiel's naked body face down to the
massage table. She laughed then slapped him on his caramel
buttock as he screamed. Diamond twittered, "Oh, it's not that

bad. A pretty little booty like yours? I'm sure you've been penetrated before."

20 Years Ago

"He doesn't even know what that means!" Lauren defended her son. Her lip quivered in fear. For a moment, she looked Ezekiel directly in his large wet brown eyes. She knew when her husband was this drunk that he was virtually unstoppable.

"Let me explain it to him then," Fred's voice dropped an octave as his lips coiled with disgust. "Do you want to suck dick?"

"Fred, stop," Lauren begged. This behavior was all too familiar. She just needed to get him into the bed. In the morning, he would never remember his actions. She urged, "Maybe if you spent some more time with him, he'd learn…"

"A man is not something you have to learn to be! You either are, or you aren't," he countered before he turned to Ezekiel with a threatening, twisted brow. "You want me to spend more time with him? Here's a test my father gave to me."

Fred slammed the glass of warm brown liquid into Ezekiel's lap and ordered, "Finish my whiskey. Ezekiel hated the smell of liquor, and even more, he hated how obnoxious it made his father.

Filled with fright and doubt, Ezekiel shook his head and refused, "I-I can't."

"Man-up!" he screamed. The heavy-set man snatched the glass out of Ezekiel's hand and pulled the boy's head backward with the other. His grip was tight as he commanded, "Drink it!"

Ezekiel shrieked like a piglet. It was like drinking fire. Tears gushed from his eyes as the harsh taste of whiskey ignited his throat.

"Stop!" Lauren begged and grabbed Fred's arm, but he batted her away like a gnat. She fell to the stained tile floors as Ezekiel began to vomit. In a fit of drunken anger, Fred sent a swift kick into the woman's stomach. Her scream was much louder than Ezekiel's and twice as earsplitting. Fred looked back at Ezekiel while the boy coughed and struggled to gain his composure. A smug curve ran across his lips, and with a chuckle, he continued to stomp his wife, "This is how you be a man."

"Mom…"

Chapter 13: Fire Ring 7: Healing and Hope

> "There shall be one law for the native and for the stranger who sojourns among you."
> **Exodus 12:49**

Once Ezekiel fell into his trance Aurora knew she was next. Brother Bainbridge hovered to her, and the second he was close enough, she lunged at him with all of the strength she had left. However, before she made contact, Diamond had already snatched her from behind.

"Now, now, little one," the man's voice was as cold as stone, "what's wrong?"

Aurora had never felt so weak, but her blind anger motivated her lips to speak, "This spa sucks. The second I get my hands on a computer, I'm going to Yelp you assholes right back to Hell."

Diamond forced Aurora onto the massage table and secured her binds while she ordered, "Keep mouthing off, and I will strangle you with your own hair."

"You better not *ever* touch my hair," Aurora spat venomously.

"Fallen angel," Bainbridge spoke softly, "do not resist. Give heed to my…"

"Never!" Aurora refused and jolted in her bind but was unable to move a centimeter. "You put your thing anywhere near me, and I swear I'll bite it off!"

"But madam, you have yet to try your new treatment," he said before he shoved the long sharp silver wand into her backside. "Here, we offer individualized acupuncture. Trust me; you need it."

14 Years Ago

"Excuse me? Hang out tonight? With you?" Aurora scoffed condescendingly as her teenage colleagues giggled behind her. Karen was the heaviest teenager in high school, but she was the only person Aurora felt comfortable shedding her secrets to. They had known each other for years, but because of Aurora's mother's distaste and high school politics, it was a relationship cloaked in mystery.

Over the years, the pair impeccably shrouded their flourishing friendship with frequent conferences in the girl's restroom and coded notes in the library. Aurora had always felt guilty that she needed to keep their relationship private, but Karen was a good sport, she understood.

Aurora worked hard to get herself into a crowd her mother approved of. She was surrounded by adolescent teens who flaunted their money, dressed like much older ladies of the evening, and had the brains of Amazonian dictators. Each gesture had to be heavily calculated.

Rebecca Haith referred to her daughter as her "second coming," and her expectations were kept very high. Remorse dominated Aurora, and she consistently denied her own emotions due to her mother's guidance. After all these years of privacy, Aurora and her best friend had finally screwed up.

Aurora narrowed her lips, and her hand drew to her waist. Karen puckered her mouth and watched Aurora with large pitiful eyes. It was the wrong place and the wrong time. The raven-haired youngster had planned the playdate with Karen almost a week ago; however, surrounded by the glam-squad of Peatmoth High, she could never admit to partying with someone as poorly dressed.

Karen was not only Aurora's best friend but almost her family. However, Karen knew the rules; they were not to speak at school. How could she forget? Karen twirled her dirty blonde hair around her finger; it was something she did when she was nervous.

Ivanna and Sasha placed their hands on their hips as they impatiently waited for Aurora to continue.

"As if I would ever be caught dead with a girl like you," Aurora was reluctant but spat venomously. She had gotten very good at lying, and the insults smoothly rolled off her tongue. Aurora's voice grew to a small roar and alerted the entire hallway, "You have the style of a homeless, blind grandmother and the body shape of a manatee pregnant with your brother's mutant triplets! What's your name? Karen? Everyone knows you are a troglodyte! Never talk to me again!"

Adrenaline raged quickly through her veins. Aurora had never been this mean to anyone, far less the one she loved the most. Her heart sank into her stomach, but her words of malice were enough to satisfy the cutthroat audience. Sasha and Ivanna laughed so hard they needed to hold each other for support. Their cackles faded away as Aurora was almost frozen when she connected regretful eyes with Karen. Tears rushed to the blonde's round face, and in a second, she was as red as a stop sign.

Remorse bathed through Aurora like sludge through empty pipes. She felt ill inside. Instantly, she understood that she had committed a grave mistake. What had she done to her best friend? Before Aurora could comfort her, Karen retreated down the hallway in a fit of tears.

"Good job at getting rid of that creep!" Ivanna congratulated.

"What did you call her?" Sasha managed to speak through outbursts of laughter. "A 'troglodyte' or something?"

"Yeah," Aurora sighed and fought back the compulsion to cry. She knew there would be no way she would ever be able to repair her friendship with Karen. "It's something my mom used to say."

"Well, I just think you're awesome," Ivanna beamed as she complimented. "You just earned yourself an invitation to Demetria's party! I wasn't supposed to tell you about it, but now I'm telling you about it." Ivanna chuckled, "Demetria will trip after she hears about what you said to that fat cow."

Chapter 14: Fire Ring 8: The List of Victims

"When man began to multiply on the face of the land and daughters were born to them, the sons of God saw that the daughters of man were attractive. And they took as their wives any they chose. Then the Lord said, "My Spirit shall not abide in man forever, for he is flesh: his days shall be 120 years." The Nephilim were on the earth in those days, and also afterward when the sons of God came into the daughters of man, and they bore children to them. These were the mighty men who were of old, the men of renown."

Genesis 6:1-4

Neil was last in line. Helplessly, in the corner of his mind, somehow, he felt his teammates suffer agonizing memories. Neil clung to what was left of himself. With every drop of blood he drank from Brother Bainbridge, his mind became foggier. Thought was impossible to form. He had never felt so victimized, not since he was a child.

Diamond strapped Neil to the table and kissed him on the cheek. There was no fight left in him. He was hungry and confused. He had no idea which devilish acts Brother

Bainbridge had planned, but he was almost at a point where he didn't care. Diamond winked flirtatiously.

"Something tells me he likes to be probed. This one is a freak. What is it with these angels and getting stuck with long pointed objects?" Diamond asked.

20 Years Ago

"I know how sad you're going to be," Katharine Qin ran her fingers through her son's chestnut hair. Neil was in bed, surrounded by fluffy pillows. His mother was extremely protective of him as he was the only child. As a super parent, Katharine was very involved in her son's life. It was no mystery why he was the perfect child. Fantastic grades, astonishing athletic achievements, and a well-respected reputation. Katharine was very proud of herself as a mother. It was her reason to live. She wanted to protect him from everything, but she failed to save him from chickenpox.

Katharine cooed softly, "You've never missed service…"

"Time to cut the cord Katharine," Donald muttered and took his wife's hand, then pulled her from Neil's bed.

"We'll only be gone a few hours. He's old enough to be alone for that long."

"I'll be fine; I'm just going to sleep anyway," Neil nodded as he pulled the sheets over his face to hide his pride. His plan was working. Excited, he hid his grin and anxiously awaited for his scheme to pull through.

With a pouty lip, his mother was dragged away by her frowning husband. Sunday service attendance was a requirement in the Qin household, and just because Neil had chickenpox, there was no reason why his parents couldn't leave him alone for a short while. Dressed in their best, Donald and Katharine regrettably got in their car and left their only child.

Neil had grown to recognize the sound of the car exiting the driveway. Electricity energized his limbs as he hopped out of bed and threw open his closet door. There Victoria stood; she was as beautiful as ever. Platinum blonde with cherry lips, she was the most developed girl in the school and the desire of every teenage boy's desire. Victoria walked out of the closet as though she was comfortable with these secretive exploits.

"Are they finally gone?" Victoria asked as she popped her gum with an exhausted, overplayed attitude. He nodded. She walked directly to Neil's bed as if she owned it and sat with her legs crossed. She asked, "What do you want to do?"

"I-I figured we could raid my parent's bar?" Neil nervously suggested.

Upon Victoria's request, Neil turned up the music. Victoria stood up from the brown leather couch and began to dance. She dipped and twirled with a sexuality Neil had only witnessed in music videos. Victoria whipped and winked as she brought Neil the NewsDay mug. Neil had never been drunk before; however, he realized a new sense of freedom with every sip of vodka. His vision blurred, but he felt so uninhibited. Rules didn't matter, and the more he broke them, the more it impressed her.

Victoria guzzled shot after shot without losing poise. She and Neil jumped on the couch to the music as the alcohol burned their throats. The blonde cupped her hand around Neil's buttock and pulled him closer. His reactions were delayed, but the pounding in his chest kept him aware. Neil's lower lip dribbled, and his eyes watched with deadpan glaze.

It was unusually hot in Augeas City Church. Though fans blew directly on Donald and Katharine, they needed to fan themselves to keep from sweating through their Sunday best. The church was filled to the max capacity, and the extra body heat added to the summer humidity. Father Brushfier gave a stiff but lengthy sermon as usual. Katharine loved his deep and smooth voice; it always gave her the chills. She allowed her eyes to blink to a close as she took her husband's hand in hers. Her heart bloomed; church always brought bliss to her life.

A crash, like an echoing rockslide, sounded so ferociously the room shook. Brief moments of confused silence washed over, but before Katharine could open her eyes, she felt the heat. An older woman dressed in a floral screeched as her face reddened and lit up with fear.

The choir scurried, and the ceiling cracked. Fire poured into the church like a cereal into a bowl. Yelps like piglets bounced off the fiery walls as the altar boys were the first to become engulfed by the hungry flames. Then the choir as they fled in terror.

Red hot air consumed the large wooden cross that hung above the stage and the white flowers surrounding it. Driven by instinct, Donald threw his arms around his wife as the blazing gas swept the church.

"Do you want to fuck me?" Victoria whispered as the music died. Her voice incited him. Adrenaline shoved pins through his spine. She drew in closer to Neil, and her squeeze had gotten tighter around his hips when she confessed. "All the boys do."

Neil bit his lower lip. He wanted to taste her body so severely he could not speak. Unsure what to do, he nodded slowly. Victoria instantly understood the signal and jumped like a tiger released from a cage. Expertly she connected to Neil's face. He could hardly hear the music over the beat of his heart. Was he really going to have sex? Was it going to be with the most beautiful girl in school?

Victoria was an artist; with little help from Neil, she laid him onto the couch and removed his shirt. He struggled to keep up with her swift lips, so Victoria grew impatient and removed her own blouse. She was wearing a sea-green bra and bounced on him like a child on a pogo stick.

Neil had no idea how to unhook a bra, but he could still feel her body. He repaid her squeezes by grabs at her breasts as she unzipped his pants. Neil had never been so excited. Slowly, he removed her jeans and slid her white panties past her thigh.

Within seconds the entire church was swallowed by hot red-orange tongues. Donald threw his wife to the ground and covered her with his body. The crash of the inferno overpowered the screams of the Christians.

Paintings of saints blackened while the piano charred. Books were turned to ash, and pews exploded. The smell of blood, burnt hair, and gas filled the room. In complete despair, Donald looked up from his wife. Ms. Osman's purple dress was scorched, and only half of it remained. Her large purple hat and curly gray hair burned a crisp black.

Mr. Petterson, their neighbor, was next to fall immersed in the blazing death. Then there was that voice.

That voice that brought Katharine so much serenity was heard like never before.

Katharine watched as Father Brushfier let out a terrible bellow as he flaked away in the intense holocaust. As the flames grew uncontrollable and the church fell apart, Donald knew there was nothing he could do. He held his wife's hand as the fire licked his flesh.

Crickets chirped a familiar tune as nighttime creatures hunted throughout Prospect Park. Not many people jogged this late at night, but Giselle had nothing to worry about. She wore a purple tracksuit, and her blonde hair was pulled up in a ponytail. Legnanu was fast asleep and gave this full-time mother a chance to ease her mind and body with a quick exercise. At her side was her fluffy brown Pomeranian ecstatic just to be outside of the house.

With the Alpha Omega dissembled, the world was going to change pretty soon. Already, the Seals' opening unleashed hellish energies, which caused the natural order of the world to unfold. Finally, things were going her way. Typhon was back, and they could finally be a family again. It was centuries before she had last seen her husband. Typhon had been sealed by a foolhardy angel and trapped beneath the earth. She tried for eons to break the bind but never could.

So Giselle was happy to surrender her unique services to Nathaniel Robinson in exchange for her husband's release. And now that Nathaniel had gotten so close with the Hidden Eye, she knew that he was her link to ultimate power and protection in the New World Order.

Nights such as these were soon to come to an end, and Giselle knew to enjoy them while they lasted. As she jogged through the empty park, Cerberus became distracted and howled loudly at a wooden bench. She stopped right in her tracks and accidentally snapped a fallen twig with her tiny tennis shoes.

Trustingly, she followed her dog's lead until the puppy circled under the bench and received a shiny pair of keys from the brush. Cerberus was very excited with his find, but Giselle was a bit confused as she picked them up. Two silver keys with a kitten charm. Upon closer inspection, the keychain had a tag on it that read, "Amanda Randall. 536 Layette Ave, Apt 3S."

Giselle took a strong whiff of the keys.

The Alpha Omega. Were they still alive? She placed the keys in her pocket. They had to die. Giselle thanks her pup, "Oh, sweetheart! You're right; this does smell like an angel!"

Chapter 15: How Do I Feel?

"Do not neglect to show hospitality to strangers, for thereby some have entertained angels unawares."

Hebrews 13:2

Typically, the hospital attendants prohibited guests from visiting patients after hours, but they had a special relationship with the New York City police department. As Martin tottered down the empty dim-lit hallway, the scent of cleaning chemicals rushed into his nose. Once again, his asthma hit. The weakening blow nearly caused him to drop his briefcase. He grabbed his chest and took a moment to compose himself.

This was nothing compared to previous recurrences and lasted only long enough for him to be reminded of his downfalls. He would never be where he was in his life or career if it hadn't been for Rhion. He knew deep down that he wasn't smart or fast, only lucky.

Martin worked relentlessly and still found nothing regarding Rhion's assault. He spent the week interviewing witnesses and today's promising lead was just another unfortunate flop.

Martin and Rhion were partners, but their lives had been intertwined for years. Their wives and children were inseparable, and vacations were incomplete without the other man present to pass a beer. Though his body ached and the lack of sleep made him irritable, he was responsible as the godfather of Rhion's twin sons to bring their father's attacker to justice.

Regrettably, Martin placed a meaty hand around the chilly silver doorknob and entered Rhion's room. It looked as though Rhion were covered with a brown wooly blanket for a split second, but upon closer inspection, the hairs on Martin's arms stood pin-straight.

Rhion was covered in a swarm of clicking cockroaches. Martin almost vomited. He had never seen anything like it; the hundreds of chestnut water bugs were all over an inch long. Viciously they bit at Rhion's flesh until they drew blood. Martin charged forward in a fit of courage and used the blanket to shake off as many starving insects as he could. However, as fast as he flicked off a roach, two more relentless vermin took their place. An onslaught of cockroaches crawled from the ceilings and under Martin's light blue button-up t-shirt.

They gnawed while they scurried on his chocolate flesh and sapped up his blood like sponges with legs. Their tiny sharp teeth felt like hot pins in his skin. Martin frantically beat his chest and squashed the creatures beneath his shirt. He screamed for the nurse.

Moments later, Doctor Devanne Kapoor rushed into the room. Young for a physician, Devanne had a fresh, caring face with a smile that could change the world. Small framed with long brown hair, red skin, and modest rectangular glasses, the woman responded with genuine concern.

"Oh my god!" Devanne exclaimed as she reached into the cupboard and retrieved a tall can of bug spray. She unleashed the poisonous gust over the insects then passed a broom to Martin. As she backed up, he squashed any roach that so much as wiggled a leg. It took three solid minutes, but once all the insects were either killed or hidden, Devanne fell into a plastic chair in exhaustion and relief.

"What the hell kind of hospital is this lady?!" Martin debased the doctor.

"I…." she tried to speak, but the doctor was out of breath. "I assure you we do everything in our power to keep a clean and safe environment."

"I beg to differ," said Martin and folded his arms.

"I don't know," Devanne folded her arms too and admitted, "strange things have been happening here lately. Things you wouldn't believe. Stillbirths that miraculously come back to life… the spreading flu we don't know how to cure or control and…M-my poor sister… gobbled up by her students."

"That was your sister? I heard about that," he apologized and rested a hand on hers. "I'm sorry."

Devanne's eyes met his for a moment, but then she looked away before she spoke. "Survivors of… fatal injuries. They'd be so…. doped up out of their minds, and they'd walk in here with gunshot wounds to the head…Missing vital organs… Maybe even carrying their own arms with their teeth. We'd operate… do the best we could, and they'd leave here alive, but in a fit of anger before the police have a chance to obtain them. We cannot keep anyone who doesn't want to be helped. I-I don't know what's going on. I don't know how they manage to get away from the police…. Ever think the world could be ending?"

"Yeah, no," he answered. "You sound like my partner. There's a reasonable explanation for all of this…"

"Roaches? I never knew them to attack people this way," she sighed with denial.

"They're roaches, doc," Martin snarled. "They can do whatever they want."

"I'll… get someone to clean up," she whispered and retreated; the click of Devanne's heels echoed down the hallway.

Martin examined Rhion's body. He was still breathing. The cool rush of relief bathed over him as he took Rhion's hand into his. They had been through so much; he knew Rhion couldn't let it end like this. He matched Rhion's long slow breaths with his, and just before he let go, the grip got tighter. Martin's jaw dropped, but before words could escape, Rhion's eyes opened with such an intense and overwhelmed vigor that Martin was brought to tears. Rhion shot upward like a spring, and Martin embraced him. His partner, his friend, was back.

Though Olive wasn't a neat freak, she could hardly stand the state of the apartment. Since Amanda had gone missing, taking care of Purrson had become a full-time job. Though the eight-legged Maine coon had the tough exoskeleton of a steel lobster, he still grew tons of hair and shed profusely.

Despite his eighteen pounds of lean muscle, extra appendages, and eyes, it took him a while to get used to his surroundings. As he became more comfortable in his skin, he grew to explore his home, leaving a trail of spider webs and cat hair wherever he went.

Olive bit her already chipped aqua green nails nervously as she placed a large map onto the living room floor. A cold chill passed through the room… the air conditioner. Was she in over her head? Hesitantly, she used an old paintbrush to draw a black triangle onto the parchment. Her heart thumped readily below her green vest as she finished her painting by detailing an eye in the center of the shape. This had to work. She had googled it. This was the best way to find Amanda.

As a roommate for several years, Olive saw Amanda as family. The girls were inseparable and shared not only a home but a life together. That was until Amanda received her angelic abilities. This was one thing they could never share. Olive was left behind as Amanda battled on to fulfill her grandiose destiny.

Alone, but she was still impressive. She was the only human who knew of Amanda's secret. That had to count for something. She refused to be helpless. Olive knew that it was her responsibility to find Amanda, even if she had to seek unconventional ways to do it.

Olive suspected that some form of demonic magic took Amanda, so why not use magic to find her? She ripped out some blonde hairs from Amanda's brush and placed them into the center of the eye she had drawn on the map. With a hesitant shrug, she lit the seventy-five dollar black Nataero candle she had bought off eBay and dripped its wax onto the center of the eye, covering Amanda's hair.

She had no idea what was supposed to happen or how this was supposed to work, but Olive had seen magic right before her eyes; she knew it existed. Purrson was living proof. Black wax drizzled onto the map and glued Amanda's hair to it. Several minutes passed by, and Olive woefully poured the syrupy, inky liquid onto the paper.

There was no glow or distortion like when Amanda used her abilities. No explosion, fire, or light show. All she could do was wait.

Two and a half hours later, the candle burnt out, and Olive dropped the disappointing heap of wax to the floor. Her green eyes rolled deep into the back of her head as she was overwhelmed with humility. Embarrassed that she believed her own foolishness, she began to clean up after the mess. Until there was a knock on the door. A pause. Then the lock started to unbolt slowly.

"Amanda…?" the woman desperately turned towards the entrance. Purrson stood on the tips of his claws and hissed suspiciously. The door swung open with such a force it left a hole in the wall. Olive jumped backward as a stranger smiled at her.

"Sorry, I just figured I'd let myself in." At the entryway stood a smaller blonde with perfectly styled hair that curled up at the bottom in large ringlets. She wore a polka-dot sundress and a white cardigan with a pink flower pin. In one hand, she held a small baby carriage and a dog leash with a tiny Pomeranian at her side, and in the other was a freshly baked pie.

Olive rolled her eyes, and her annoyance pervaded in every word she spoke, "Excuse me! How did you get in here?"

"Hello there!" Giselle greeted. "Sorry, just to drop by like this, but we're the new family in the neighborhood, and I just thought it might be nice to get to know some of y'all!" Her voice dropped an octave. It was strong and deep but clear as it rang with a southern accent, "*Let me in.*"

Involuntarily, Olive had lost control of her body and stepped aside as Giselle entered the room. Her voice was still cold and dark, "*Lock the door behind you and have a seat.*"

Olive's stomach imploded, and a chill ran to her very bones. Her mind had betrayed her. Like a dog, she listened. She wanted to obey. Olive locked the front door and fell into a corner as Giselle placed her baby's carrier on the kitchen counter.

"Hsssss!" Purrson flew across the room and scurried beneath the couch.

"Sorry to greet you here with the whole cavalry, but you know a mother's work is never done. Do you have kids?" She looked around in disgust and concluded, "No… it doesn't look like you do; this place is a bit untidy." Her giggle was as sweet as vanilla pudding, "Anyway, sometimes, I just don't know how I do it all. I had to find time to walk Cerberus, pack lunch for the twins, take Aros to her ascension; it's really been a busy day. Can someone explain to me why I was put on house call duty twice this week? I do have a family to raise after all. But I have to admit; it is nice to get out of the house every once in a while and get to know some new people."

"H-how did you do that?" Olive managed to ask as her heart exploded in her chest and her eyes flooded with water. "Who are you?"

"Depends on who you ask," Giselle simpered sweetly as she took Cerberus off his leash and started to wash her hands in the kitchen sink, "You humans used to call me 'Echidna'… before that, it was 'Lilith.' But now, I go by Giselle. So ethnic!"

"Okay…" Olive's fingers tightened around her skirt when she asked, "What do you want? A-are you some sort of angel? I didn't summon you."

"Oh no, not exactly, no one I know would ever answer a call this weak. However, I did find some keys with this odor on them, and my-my, it does smell like an angel in here, doesn't it? Your little call just made it all the easier to confirm, that's all!" Giselle answered as she placed Amanda's keys on the countertop. She then took a fist full of Olive's red hair and threw her across the room as quickly as she would sprinkle grass seeds on a lawn. "Don't worry; I have a solution for that scent! Two parts Pine-Sol, one part vinegar! Trust me, there's no smell that vinegar can't neutralize! You'll have your place smelling like a meadow by morning!" she concluded. "Until then, us girls can just gossip! Where do you keep your wine?"

Olive groaned as she crumbled in the corner and weakly positioned her thin-framed glasses back on her face.

"Never mind." Gracefully, Giselle fished wine glasses out of the cabinet then poured Merlot, "So darling, you have to tell me. How does a human-like you know an angel?"

"Are you a demon?"

"Honey," Giselle cooed as she knelt beside Olive and shoved the glass of warm red wine into her hand. The blonde smelt like custard and freshly cut flowers. She almost sang while she spoke, "In this neighborhood, names and titles mean nothing. Power is all anyone is interested in."

"I didn't summon you," Olive reluctantly mumbled as she took the glass.

"No," Giselle agreed and walked over to the spell Olive had started on the living room floor. She picked up Amanda's blonde hair and sniffed it before she began to set the dinner table. Her poise was impeccable, and her elegance was masterful, yet Olive could taste something dark within this woman. She continued, "Your spell didn't do so well. Nowadays, there is no angel, fallen or otherwise, that would answer a call this weak, but this hair. This isn't any normal angel you were summoning, was it? I found the same scent on these keys."

"Why do you need to know?" Olive finally found the strength to speak. Her eyes were wide, deep, warm with salty water. "You just show up at my doorstep, force your way in, and you expect me to trust you?"

"*Come to the table*," Giselle commanded, and Olive was obligated to follow. The blonde cut the lukewarm, juicy red pie into eighths and placed a slice into a smaller plate. She served Olive, then herself, and sat across from her. "*Eat.*"

Reluctantly, Olive took the fork between her fingers. The pie was bitter and had hints of lead and copper. Olive immediately spit the pastry out only seconds after she had tasted it. Repulsed, she asked, "What is that?"

"You know I met your neighbor today! I came by earlier, and you weren't home." Giselle swallowed a fork full of the crusty pie and neatly wiped her mouth with a napkin, and continued, "But I followed your scent next door. I met this delightful lady. Short, brunette, polite! I knew she was a kind woman, but I didn't think she would be so sweet."

"What?" Olive cried out before she tried to jump from her chair. "M-my sister?"

"Your sister! Oh, is that why you both smelled alike! I knew it was some sort of connection. You live next to your sister? My, you two must have been so close?" Giselle giggled. "*Eat*," the blonde commanded in her dark, echoed voice. Helpless, Olive lost control of her body. Under Giselle's command, she picked up the fork and stabbed it into her slice of the pie.

"Now, you see, I know it can be a little intimidating when someone new moves into the neighborhood, but you don't have to be defensive. We can be friends! I made you this pie, didn't I? With a little bit of help from your sister, I just wanted it to be perfect. It's because I care." Giselle snickered.

Fireworks exploded in her mind. Was she eating her sister?

Giselle casually went on, "You know I can make you tell me exactly what I want to hear, but I figured since this was our first time meeting, we might as well make it memorable! So tell me, how do you know an angel?"

"I-I was roommates with one," Olive felt empty but answered. Fear and sadness paralyzed her. She was in shock and cried through the mouthfuls of the bloody pie. "S-she went missing…"

"What was her name?" Giselle blinked when she asked.

"Amanda Randall," she swallowed spoonfuls of her dead sister while she responded.

"Now, isn't that Raphael?" Giselle asked and inched to the edge of her seat. Giselle's infant child started to cry. The woman rolled her eyes and rushed to Legnanu. She took him into her arms and rocked him slowly, with a crooked grin on her face. "The Alpha Omega? They're no longer a problem. But that's good to know she still has some earthly connections… They probably should die sooner than later. *Finish up your pie,* now."

Olive's eyes burned with tears as she shoved forkfuls of her sister's corpse into her mouth. Defeated and broken, blood dripped down the sides of Olive's mouth. She could not control her body, but she could control her mouth, "You sick bitch. You need to seek help."

Giselle batted her large blue eyes for a few seconds, and she rocked her crying child, he confessed.

"Aw, I like you. And you know, you're right! Deep down, I do need help. I could absolutely use a babysitter!"

"Thank you for coming." Elisa appreciated the cop as she sluggishly allowed Martin to enter her home. She had huge black circles under her eyes. Though she tried, she could not shake the tension from her shoulders. It was late, and the children were in bed; however, her husband was full of energy. The brunette was wearing a pink robe over a baggy t-shirt and a pair of Rhion's checkered boxers. She sighed heavily and walked Martin to the stained white living room couch.

"No problem," Martin said, and he collapsed into the chair as Elisa sat daintily beside him. "How is he?"

"Not so good," Elisa admitted, "he's convinced the city is full of devils. Real ones." Elisa held back her shameful tears, "He thinks they're after him and us."

Martin paused for a moment; he remembered Rhion was suspicious of the supernatural, but he never took it seriously. The heavyset man took in a lung full of air then scratched his mustache, "PTSD is common with police officers after they go through something like this. Can I talk to him?"

Elisa led Martin up the stairs and into their bedroom. There, wearing red pajama pants and a white tee, Rhion stood on a dresser and reached toward the ceiling fan. As Martin and Elisa entered the room, Rhion jumped down and approached them with apprehensiveness.

His chestnut hair was disheveled; his green eyes were tired. Dried perspiration gave his skin a sour whiff, and his grin was crooked with anxiety. Rhion cleared his throat and asked happily, "Is it time to get back to work?"

Martin slowly shook his head as he answered, "No. Not yet. How are you doing, pal?"

"I'm fine," Rhion retorted and narrowed his brow defensively, then frowned suspiciously. "So, what did you come here for?"

"I heard you're having some trouble sleeping," Martin continued.

Rhion folded his arms and spat defensively, "I know what I saw, Martin. I'm not crazy."

"It's just…" the policeman searched for words, "Sometimes when things like this happen to us, we can be a little unclear."

"Oh," Rhion scoffed, "I'm clear. I was on to something. That's why Neil Qin tried to kill me!"

"Oh, Rhion…" Elisa whimpered. When her husband got this way, she knew there was little she could do to derail him.

"He isn't human," Rhion revealed. "He used his telekinetic abilities to put me in a coma."

"Telekinesis isn't real," Elisa doubted him. She folded her arms and closed her eyes. It was difficult to even look at this man anymore.

"I saw it!" Rhion bellowed, and his voice bounced throughout the house like a gunshot in a narrow alley.

"Calm down, buddy," Martin cautioned. "Even if what you say is true, what are you going to do about it?"

"I need to protect my family and this city from monsters like him," Rhion snarled as his fingers formed a determined fist. "One man with that kind of power… What is stopping him from walking into the White House and ripping it to shreds? Or… Or killing us all with a thought?"

"Don't be a conspiracist!" Martin interjected. "The attack was from al-Qaeda or something. They killed the president. Neil has *been* missing. We assume he's dead."

"Why would you assume he's dead? He's hiding!" Rhion disagreed, then gritted his teeth and ran his fingers through his thick brown-black hair. "I need to get back on the force. I'm not crazy… I just need some time to prove it."

"If you're not crazy…" Martin rubbed the shoulders of his ex-partner, "then stop talking about this…"

Chapter 16: Is This All There Is?

"So then you are no longer strangers and aliens, but you are fellow citizens with the saints and members of the household of God"
Ephesians 2:19

Neil would never admit it, but Brother Bainbridge's powers were considerably strong. The demon claimed to be the most powerful psychic on the Western Hemisphere, and deep down, Neil knew it was true. From the first time Bainbridge entered his mind, Neil was utterly taken over. Bainbridge dug up deep-rooted memories that Neil thought he forgot eons ago.

Sorrow was reintroduced to the forefront of his psyche and fogged his thoughts and direction. Neil knew Bainbridge distracted him to brainwash him, but he was helpless to the influence. He took short deep breaths and watched as the small gray Z'New demons guarded his cell.

The angel could feel Bainbridge watching. Bainbridge was very keen on interpreting brain frequencies and expected Neil to contact the rest of his team. But… what if that's not who he wanted to contact? Neil was exhausted and knew he could never reach Sister Lyssah Rhamiel from this distance.

However, there was one other spirit in the building that didn't taste downright evil. He closed his eyes in centralization. It felt like he walked barefoot on broken glass. With Bainbridge around to detect him, he had to use his powers with caution. Like a burst of electricity through a motherboard Neil released a mental beacon into the ether. His consciousness zipped through the air, and within moments he was in the mind of Diamond Love.

The room was half the size of Neil's apartment and looked over three times more expensive. An oversized window revealed the sleepless city and allowed its milky light to cast a glow onto the aged dark oak floor. Clean white towels were rolled up neatly beside fluffy robes and iced water with lemon and mint. Lavish paintings of archaic owls, Egyptian pyramids, immense, oval green eyes, and torches decorated the peach-colored walls.

Neil could smell the burning incense and fragrant bowl of potpourri as if he were physically in the room. Lit candles of various lengths flickered across the tall bamboo plants and a spotless bathtub, where Diamond soaked in a sea of pink bubbles.

"Well," Neil uttered when he cleared his throat, "this is nice."

Diamond's eyes were like icy needles. "How did you get in?" she started but paused, then snarled exasperatedly. "Oh. You're in my mind. God, I hate you mind things. Ugh, how are you even doing this mind projection thing? You're supposed to be weakened."

"I just wanted to see how the other side lived." Neil walked to the window and gazed at the blinking traffic lights for a brief moment. "This is a really nice spa. Except for the basement, of course."

"I'm calling Bainbridge," Diamond announced as she sloshed around in the porcelain tub beneath the massive illustration of a serpent that ate its own tail. She explained, "Tell him that his stupid white lights aren't working anymore..."

"Wait," the angel urged. "I don't think you want to do that. I-I can feel it in you. You have a soul, just like me."

"I sold my soul," she sarcastically confessed as she sank back into the tub and allowed the water to barely cover her breasts, "don't act like you know a damn thing about me."

"I don't need to know much to know that you understand the difference between right and wrong," Neil retorted. "You *have* a conscience."

"Having a conscience doesn't pay the bills," Diamond quipped as she washed some fizz off her ankle and revealed a small ankh tattoo. "I work for the supreme being, Brother Bainbridge and the Hidden Eye now."

"So is it money you want then?" His nose wrinkled with disgust when he questioned her. "I can help you with that. But I don't think that's what you want…"

"Oh?" she gasped sneeringly, then raised an eyebrow.

"I think you're trapped here just like us," Neil hypothesized as he took in the luxurious room and sighed. "Well, maybe not just like us. But you're a prisoner too. We could help each other. Who is keeping you here?"

"This little mind thing you're doing," Diamond hissed and pointed a long red fingernail at the man, "it's cute, but from where I'm sitting, it doesn't look like you can help me at all."

"You're just a human; I can show you great things," Neil suggested. "I can get you out of here, free all of us."

With an expression as bitter as a tundra, Diamond rose from the bathtub. Leisurely, she allowed her long black hair to slink over her shoulders as soapy water ran off her shape and make puddles at her feet. The busty woman approached Neil while he stood naked in her mind. She lifted her ivory palm and flashed the silver signet she wore. Her sultry stare was chilling, and her pink lips puckered as she spoke, "This is the Seal of Solomon. This ring controls me, but with it…" Diamond made a fist, and Neil was forced to stand up straight by an outside power. "I can control all things. People. Animals. Demons. Shit with and without souls. I've seen some pretty great things," Diamond took a tight handful of Neil's genitals then informed him, "and you aren't one of them."

She pressed her lips against his, and he failed to resist. He was chewing gum in her mouth. Neil's knees buckled, and he grabbed the sides of her head as he shoved her tongue into her. Diamond had an overpowering sexual allure. It was a skill she obtained early in life and mastered throughout the years. Just as Neil enveloped her with his muscular thighs, she yanked at a fist full of his greasy hair and ordered, "Now get out."

Neil's physical body absorbed his psyche like a metal rod took lightning. He was charged but had nowhere to go. Back in his cramped, hot room, he was once again alone.

Aurora lost sensation in her legs. As though her bones had turned to marshmallow, she stammered then stumbled to the ground. As the Angel of Time and Destiny, Aurora could see into the future; however, the visually impairing fluorescent lights severely drained her power.

A single tear descended past her cheek. Though she could not muster enough strength to see into the future, she could see into the present. She awoke from her vision with more pain than when she fell into it. What was Neil doing? Just when she trusted him, how could he betray her? How could he kiss that… demon? Not only did she see it? She felt it. She fought the urge to vomit. He wanted her; desired that demon!

But wait, she wasn't a demon, the ankh tattoo on her leg. Ezekiel said that meant life, human. Aurora dried her eyes and wrapped her arms around her stomach. Maybe there was a way out of this prison. All she needed to do was to come up with a plan.

Puffy circles grew dark around Olive's eyes. Giselle had a sick sense of humor and never allowed Olive any sleep. With only the sound of her voice, Giselle repeatedly forced Olive to accomplish vile tasks according to her will. Olive's fingernails were caked with soil from when she helped Giselle plant human heads in flowerpots, and her skin was a sickly yellow as Giselle drained Olive's blood then made her drink it. Water welled in her eyes for the horrors she had witnessed but was forced to endure.

She was cold. Her body trembled with memories of Legnanu playing in deer organs like spaghetti, and her fingers still quivered as she was forced to sow a human-skinned quilt.

Giselle enjoyed Olive, not only because she was her slave, but she needed the company. Giselle always needed to vent. Whenever Olive would stop crying, Giselle would spark up gossip about neighborhood demons and her family problems. To her, they were a perfect match.

When Giselle was going to be distracted, Olive was forced to babysit Giselle's demonic son, Legnanu, who sat blindfolded in his carrier and usually remained silent but got heavier every day. Olive's arms were getting tired, but she dared not drop Legnanu's baby blue carriage… not at an event like this.

Olive broke into a sweat. She stopped in her tracks. Malnourished, she struggled to carry the heavy child. Her weak heartbeat pounded, and her hands felt clammy. She was Legnanu's baby bottle. For days, she was forced to feed him blood through her breasts. The infant child drank so much she could hardly stand. No thoughts entered or left her mind as her eyes widened at the assembly before her.

This was the first time Olive had seen live humans in days. For a moment, she thought she was in Hell, but seeing all these people, walking and laughing reminded Olive she was still on Earth. Hunger made her delirious, and she had no idea where the demon had brought her, but as commanded, she never spoke.

The party was held in a church unlike Olive had ever seen. Massive and ornamented like a luxury museum, Olive's senses were overloaded. Images of stoic but influential men and women were hand-painted, and the artwork hung on every wall. Each table wore an expensive ruby cloth and held ornate bouquets of red roses.

The lights were dim, and Olive's stomach protested in starvation. She could smell the juicy, buttery shrimp, almost taste the flaky quiches on the silver paltered covered in rosemary and fresh dill. Her fingers tightened around the baby's carriage. She wanted to scream out to the other humans. Beg for help!

Food, water, anything, but her lips were sealed under Giselle's magical command.

Surrounded by politicians in expensive suits, Olive tiptoed behind Giselle as the blonde beautifully greeted each senator with a warm hug and a butterfly kiss.

With a stunning vision, Giselle held her husband at his arm. They were an opposite in every sense. She was radiant perfection that smelt like a creamsicle. He, however, was dishevelment embodied. Shaggy and careless, Typhon's knotted black hair reached his lower back, and his suit was ill-fit and covered in wrinkles. He was blind but used no walking stick and wore large black glasses across his long pale face.

Nathaniel walked ahead of the couple with his frigid and forever silent, bland wife. Built like a juggernaut in a practical gray suit dress and tiny oval glasses, her step was as heavy and robust as a professional wrestler. Though much smaller than his wife, Nathaniel was still tall among the other congressmen and political figures who attended this gathering.

Gaily, honey-flavored wine flowed throughout Nathaniel's usual respectable guests. Even those who normally refrained from drinking guzzled glass after glass with little encouragement from Giselle. The more intoxicated the group became, the looser and more gleeful they felt. As the soirée commenced, it was clear that the wine had euphoric and addictive properties, but no one seemed to notice as they laughed and played with slight hallucinations, waves of light, and imaginary bubbles.

At the height of the shindig's excitement, Nathaniel confidently took to the stage. He enjoyed the sound of his voice, and in a room full of inebriated adults, he felt invincible. He cleared his throat and grabbed the microphone before he asked, "Is everyone enjoying themselves?"

The crowd cheered as he continued, "Yes, yes, I'm sure you are. You see that feeling. I bet you feel empowered. Unstoppable. Don't you? Maybe a little drunk, huh? Well, that's not just a boost of confidence you're having. The complimentary wine you're drinking, this is a special type of mixture."

"You drugged us?" someone just from the crowd. "I knew it!"

"Whoa, whoa, whoa, hold on now, it's not a drug. It's a recipe passed down in the Greek tradition for generations." Nathaniel shrugged. "It's better than any drug you've ever heard of. Liquid Gold. Or Nectar, as the kids call it. It will make you feel like a God."

Nathaniel's wife, Fran Miller Robinson, took hold of a woman in the crowd. She dragged her up to the stage and, with the ease of opening a jar of peanut butter, twisted the woman's head until her spine snapped. The assembly shrieked in horror and erupted into chaos. Nonchalantly, Nathaniel continued, "But not only will it make you feel like a God, it can make you God-like!"

The small mob started to uproar but ceased in amazement when the congresswoman's body twitched with life. Within moments the corpse cracked and jerked in uncomfortable positions until her spine was unknotted. Her eyes bulged like golf-balls. She gasped for breath as she healed completely. Confused and frightened, the woman grabbed at her body to make sure it was really there.

A wave of shock took the crowd, and when a smile crossed his thin lips, Nathaniel chuckled smugly, "Nectar will make you immortal. It will open the door to worlds never seen and sensations never felt. I am willing to offer it to you for political support and loyalty, of course."

"You drugged us," an older man rebuked, "murdered someone in front of us, then brought her back to life? What devil's business is this? I will have no part of it!"

Giselle quickly approached the elderly gentleman and whispered into his ear. Her voice was a resounding echo, *"Leave here. You're going to forget everything you've seen and heard. Go home, put down newspaper, so you don't make a mess, and stab yourself through the eye with the largest knife you can find. Don't stop cutting until all of your brains are gone. Try not to get anything on your wife's clean floor."*

Without a word, the man turned and walked out of the room. The crowd shivered in awe and disbelief. A senator raised his hand, "How do we know it's safe?"

"It's completely safe," Nathaniel continued. "We tested it on urban communities before we brought it to you, of course. No injury is beyond repair! Complete and utter immortality. Temporary, of course. But yes, go ahead. Try to kill each other. No one here can die."

"W-where did you get this from?"

"That's classified information," Nathaniel answered, then adjusted his suit jacket. "Like I said, 'a family recipe.' Now, do we have a deal?"

The congresswoman of California released a heavy breath and placed her plate of roast beef on the table. Drunk, the sixty-four-year-old woman could hardly stand, but she was overcome with a trusting euphoria that dared her to challenge logic. In an instant of venturesomeness, she violently took hold of the fork in her plate and stabbed the senator's wife in the neck.

The crowd froze. She screeched as blood sputtered out of her veins. However, milliseconds later, she stopped bleeding and plucked the fork from her neck while her body wholly healed.

Astonished and excited, the group attacked each other. Every item in the room was a weapon. Brutally, they murdered each other and watched while they died and recovered. Drunkenly, they laughed as they slit each other's throats and stabbed each other in the eyes.

"Impressive," complimented a brunette with pin-straight hair down to her backside. She approached

Nathaniel and cheered him with a half-empty glass of wine in her hand, then adjusted her sensible pantsuit as she retorted, "It reminds me of the parties Dionysus used to host."

"I'm glad you're enjoying it, Minerva," Nathaniel winked at her as he spoke. "It wouldn't be possible without you."

"I'm glad you understand that," Minerva said as she smiled. "It is a fabulous plan… power in exchange for temporary immortality. How addicting for humans, they can never resist ambrosia." She cleared her throat. "But I have a proposition: I'd like to buy that red-headed human slave from you."

"Lilith's pet?" Nathaniel chuckled. "Do you like her for some reason?"

Minerva's tiny pink lips scrunched up as she tried to hold back a smirk when she spoke, "Let's just say I like her name."

Chapter 17: Why Can't You Leave Me Alone?

Sister Lyssah Rhamiel no longer prayed. Her morals refused to let her. Concealed for centuries under a shroud of magical wards, amulets, and supernatural protection, Lyssah was a secret. Haunted by spirits from her past, she remained in constant paranoia. Everyone and practically everything wanted her dead.

Except for the Alpha Omega and Stolas the Maniae.

She could sense it and even taste their honesty and rawness. Human souls made them different from other angels. They were not only the Lord's military but his heart as well.

Though she was cut off from the world around her, she was very aware of the current events. She could touch the energy in the air and feel the emotions of children continents away from her. The gift of compassion was an ability that came with great woe. Lyssah remained in constant distress and, more than often, never knew whether an emotion was genuinely hers or one she had plucked out from the ether.

When it became overwhelming, she cut herself. Tiny and elaborate whittled scriptures, emotions, and messages she needed to keep track of. As she got older, the easier it was to forget, and the more difficult it was to nullify passionate and dangerous sentiments.

The older woman rocked slowly on her tattered yarn couch as a small gray owl fluttered into the room. Stolas the Maniae planted himself in his mother's hand. This helped center her thoughts. She funneled energy through the bird, and like a sponge, absorbed her desires. The small gray bird looked up at him with raisin eyes.

"'I'm going to that church, and you're not going to stop me. I know that Lyssah Rhamiel knows something about what's going on...'" Stolas the Maniae quoted Rhion.

It was a warning that Lyssah wished had come at least an hour sooner as a loud knock sounded at her door. The older woman brushed the bird off her hand and trotted toward the entry. She placed a wrinkled palm on the hefty wooden portals, then connected her ear.

"Sister Lyssa Rhamiel," the officer was sweating when he screamed. His shirt was unevenly buttoned, and his pants were falling off his waist. His shaggy brown hair stuck up like a sea urchin. Rhion was disheveled, but his fists were hammers on the oak. He demanded, "Let's not play this game. I know that you're in there. This is the police; open up."

Lyssah could sense his anxiety. Behind the door, he was alone, nervous. Something was not right, but she knew he would stay there forever if she waited in silence. She asked, "What do you want, officer?"

"I am Detective Rhion Galloway, and I need you to open the door, ma'am," the green-eyed man bellowed.

"You do not have a warrant," Lyssah assumed as the man was alone, "and you are not here under judicial right."

Rhion stammered a bit. How did she know? He cleared his throat and sputtered, "Ma'am, I just have a few questions about the disappearance of Neil Qin."

"I don't know him."

"I know that he's been here several times, along with Aurora Haith, Amanda Randall, and Ezekiel Wallace, all of whom are missing." Rhion breathed heavily through his nose, "Eyewitnesses recall this as the last place he had been before his disappearance and oh yeah… the mysterious gas leak that shut this place down that's oh yeah... exactly how his parents died."

"You don't care about any of that," Lyssah knew as she vocalized. "You're here for other reasons. You're looking for answers, but you're not asking the right questions…"

"And what questions would those be?"

"Is there a God? What is death? Is there pain? Is there pleasure? What is love? Who are you? Will you ever belong?" Lyssah crouched down the side of her door as she listed.

"Ma'am," Rhion groaned, "I just want to know…"

"If you can believe your eyes?" Lyssah's nails dug deep into the wood when she spoke. "If what you're seeing is real…if you're mad… or enlightened?"

"Jus—"

"I will tell you," she began. Lyssah's thin pink lips quivered as tears ran down her face. "The End of Days is among us. Reality is bleeding. Walls that separate all things melt. Believe your eyes. Dimensions are breaking, and things are getting through. You have seen the Earth weep. Tasted her salty cries, and now you know. You are not a lunatic. This world is unraveling… right before you!"

"W-what can I do?" he cried. Validation at last. Rhion's knees fell weak. For the first time, someone had justified what he had witnessed. He pressed his ear to the door and felt the message resonate within him.

"You want to know where you can find Neil?" Lyssah confessed. "The angel is at the Dianetic Hospital. He will be in a fiery cocoon. There you will find all of your missings. Murder… torture… demons. You will find a room full of killers! And the answers you seek. Bring him to me."

Rhion's heart was in his throat. He waved his fingers through his thick sweaty black-brown hair. As wasps from the small nest overruled the unkempt yard, Rhion stepped away from the door. Finally, he understood and knew what he needed to do.

"I knew you would come around," the mighty angel whizzed. Neil released a hefty burst of muggy air as his chest contracted. Sweltering pellets of moisture crawled down his torso like rainfall dripped off a windowpane.

He was trapped in his wooden prison, but his mind remained boundless. His nostrils flared and moved into a more comfortable position on the pine bench. A sanguine smile bridged his lips, and in his mind, he beheld Diamond Love in all of her glory.

The busty woman covered herself in a long fluffy robe that had a red upside-down triangle emblem on the back.

Smugly, she inched herself up on the porcelain bathtub and winked at the angel in her mind, "Well, a woman does have her needs. Have you seen this place? Nothing but Z'New demons and monster nurses; I don't have a lot of options…"

"I told you I was capable of great things," Neil boasted smugly.

"Don't get too coy with me," Diamond retorted. "Never fucked an angel before. For some reason, I thought it would feel more… I don't know… pure? But you're just as dirty as the rest of them."

"Baby," Neil muttered and was slightly insulted. Sex was never something he had to defend, and he was annoyed that she challenged him. "I could tear apart this entire building while I'm inside you."

"So why didn't you then?" Diamond questioned and raised a curious eyebrow.

"Bainbridge," the angel admitted, "he cut me off from my teammates, and if he knew I were here…"

"Bainbridge is not the boss of me," Diamond quipped defensively. She spat on the ground, "This is just a temporary gig for me. I do whatever and whoever *whenever* I want."

"That's not what you were saying before," Neil combated.

"It's what I'm saying now."

"Well, you don't know what you're missing. Right now, you're only getting me about halfway," his eyes locked in with hers as he cooed, "you turn down these lights… just a little bit, and I'll show you what a real angel can do."

"I guess I could use you if I ever run out of batteries," Diamond supposed as she tapped her front teeth with her long red nails. "Sounds nice, but how do I know you're not going to escape?"

"Because I'll be here with you," Neil announced and took Diamond into his arms, "and even if I try, I know you could put me down in two strides."

"One stride," Diamond confirmed, resting her head on his chest. She had never had intercourse with an angel, far less an angel that could have intercourse with her mind. The experience thrilled her, and her climax was like none she had ever felt before… though technically, she was the only one in the room.

"I'll turn the lights down," she agreed as she pushed his head between her legs, "but you gotta show me how you go down first."

Chapter 18: Where Can I Find understanding?

"You shall not eat anything that has died naturally. You may give it to the sojourner who is within your towns, that he may eat it, or you may sell it to a foreigner. For you are a people holy to the Lord your God. You shall not boil a young goat in its mother's milk."
Deuteronomy 14:21

Crisp bitterness whistled through bamboo wind-chimes and was gently layered by echoes of toning bowls and vibrating gongs. The spa's indoor-outdoor massive pool was cut in a decorative puzzle shaped like alongside swastikas. Lit torches hung on pillars, and their warm licks illuminated the intricate carvings on the tiles that surrounded the sparkling oasis.

Giselle pulled her husband in closer to her. Her hypnotizing sapphire eyes gazed in awe as her plump red lips parted with disbelief. The immaculateness enticed her. She smoothed out a wrinkle in her all-pink attire. Then she almost nervously pulled at her pearl necklace as she tightened her grip around Typhon's crusted long fingers.

He was calm as always. His hair was knotted into a lengthy black ponytail, and his disordered suit clung to him sloppily. He was barefoot and did not wear his usual sunglasses, so black ore dripped from his sightless pupils. The ink ran down his pale face like tears, but the crooked smile on his face revealed his joy.

"Aw, honey," Giselle cooed, "I wish you could see this place."

"I don't need to see," Typhon simpered. "Do you hear that deadly… magical sound? I haven't heard anything like it in ages. Most beautiful, a symphony between control and chaos! Up and down, never going one way or another, into the depths of the ocean or the endless stars, getting lost in something and losing everything to get lost in…"

"I am so glad you approve of my music friend," Brother Bainbridge spoke as they approached. He was eighteen feet tall. The spa owner sat at the head of the bath in a giant purple throne with his right arm extended dispassionately to his side. An extensive abrasion on his wrist opened the flow of his sugary red blood into Bainbridge's shorter gray slaves' mouths. The black-eyed creatures rushed for the fluid as though their very lives depended on it as the reptilian nurses with needles played the toning bowls and hit the gongs.

Hamster-sized bees with faces identical to Bainbridge's swarmed the air above him. In unison with the giant, they smiled a toothy grill of green pointed rowed teeth and narrowed their yellow eyes. Naked, his leathery overlapping flaps were exposed, and as Typhon and Giselle approached, Diamond Love removed her head from his crotch. She secured his red towel around his waist. Bainbridge cleared his throat and spoke, "You were always one for good taste in music… and Giselle… you're looking as lovely as ever!"

"Well, aren't you just the sweetest?" the blonde blushed as she giggled.

"Hello, Beelzebub," Typhon hummed. "It's been a long time!"

Diamond wiped her mouth with the back of her hand then threw her long black hair behind her head. "Bainbridge, who are these chumps? And don't give me that 'friends' crap. Everybody can't be your goddamn friend."

"Is that a human? You should really put a muzzle on it before I rip its little tongue out." Typhon clenched his teeth and shook his head disappointedly when he warned. "God, you disgust me; you've lost all your pizzazz! Shame. Just look at you. Feeding little versions of yourself… yourself. What are you doing working for the Hidden Eye? I thought you were the Highest Operating Psychic in Western Hemisphere. Or maybe I got that wrong. Maybe it's just the Upper West Side…"

"Come now," Bainbridge shuddered but kept his wrist held high enough for his blood to continue to rain onto his creatures. "Why the rudeness? What have I ever done to you? Once Titans... Now, aren't you working for that False Messiah?"

"*For* and *with* are two separate genres of music!" Typhon tilted his head to the side and sassed, "Which brings me to why we're here. Word on the street is that you are in control of the New Horsemen of the Apocalypse… We know they're still alive. So…. If you could just point us in that direction, we'd love to get a quick look-e-loo."

"Oh, Typhon, you little whipper-snapper," Bainbridge cautioned and shook his head slowly, "I think you already know the answer to that."

"Then bring on the orchestra!" Typhon cheered as though he had heard exactly what he wanted. Now had an excuse to let loose, "Crazed music! There is a hurricane a-blowing!"

"Oh, Typhoeus …" Giselle lovingly cooed.

Flames from the torches angled as the strong gusts of winds cracked into the room with only half a roof. Typhon arched his knees and planted his feet when a lunatic curl crossed his lips. Giselle knew this look like she knew tuna casserole. She stepped backward and covered her mouth in a coil of bashfulness. He was a dangerous genius and musician. Unkempt and as powerful as a cyclone. This is why she loved him. Needed him.

The sky began to crackle, and thunder echoed off the tiled walls. Diamond shot an apprehensive glance toward Brother Bainbridge while the sky grew even darker. She asked, "Yo, can I waste these guys?"

He nodded and agreed, "Have fun."

In an instant, Diamond snatched up a standing torch and charged the intruders. Just as she was halfway, Typhon unleashed a gale so powerful it lifted her into the air. However, before the agile woman was taken off course, she buried the steel torch into the ground, which gave her enough momentum to send a roundhouse kick into the demon's face. Typhon slid across the floor, and the harsh winds ceased.

"The Seal of Solomon! Where did you get that?" Giselle gasped as she turned to the warrior. She knew the ring very well, as their abilities were similar. It controlled bodies, and she managed minds. However, that wasn't the ring's only power. With legendary independence, the ring seemed to be a skilled master at a myriad of unique talents.

Her force was like a truck; Diamond lunged forward and slugged Giselle in the chin. Giselle's body straightened and bent under Diamond's control like a puppet. In pain, her eyes grew more comprehensive, and the blonde's voice grew deep, "*Kill yourself!*"

Diamond wiped out a pocket knife from her left boot. In a trance, she aimed it at her own neck, but before she could make contact, her right hand stopped her. It was as though the Ring of Solomon had a life and a mind of its own. The ring controlled her right arm, and they fought as though they were separate beings. The silver band overpowered Diamond's weaker hand then forced her to attack Giselle.

"We'll let the ladies duke this one out," Typhon supposed, then brushed off some soot from his dusty blue suit paints. The air became feverish. Hot winds blew in every direction and bloated dark clouds formed in the sky. Like cracked eggs, they split. A roar ripped from the above so loud that it sounded like a celestial car crash. Brightness blinded the room as it lit up with electricity, and white lightning churned from the heavens.

A bold surge struck at Bainbridge.

However, as he sat in his large chair, almost nonchalantly, a pink shield of energy protected him from the blast. Typhon jumped in excitement like a happy, wild monkey. When he leaned in, a series of lightning bolts pummeled the shaking earth.

Giselle lashed at Diamond with monstrous strength, but the Ring of Solomon moved with the agility and skill of a Ninjutsu master. Still abiding by Giselle's command,

Diamond lunged at her own face with a pocket knife; the ring was able to defend her while thrashing the blonde about. When the fight neared the pool, Giselle shouted a new command, "*Drown yourself!*"

Without hesitation, Diamond dove into the water. Before she was completely under, however, her right hand grabbed Giselle by the ankle. Giselle struggled to escape Diamond's bear trap hold but was forced underneath along with the raven-haired ring bearer.

Swarms of bees buzzed menacingly as, one by one, they flew at Typhon. Temperatures rapidly fell. Wind and hail stormed into the room, chopping up the pool water and freezing the large bees and Z'New demons to death. Bainbridge held his bleeding wrist with his other hand. His slight reptilian features grew more stern as his attention was now entirely on Typhon.

A pounding migraine entered Typhon's mind, and as he grabbed his knotted hair, small explosions sounded around him. Typhon leaped backward, but it was as if he were stepping on landmines. Reality rippled. Bubbles floated around Typhon and detonated like miniature hydrogen bombs.

Giselle lifted her head above water and desperately gasped, "Fine! *Don't drown yourself*!"

Diamond released her grasp, and the two women sprinted out of the pool. She was breathing heavily. Diamond cracked her neck so hard a puddle of water flew from her hair. Giselle was incredibly strong and would get the best of her if she didn't strike quickly. In a dash, Diamond pulled the lantern from the ground and broke it over her knee, then lunged at Giselle.

"*Kill Beelzebub*!" Giselle hollered and narrowed her blue eyes with pride. Perhaps this would work. There was no way she was going to let a prostitute with a silver ring defeat her.

Diamond had no choice. She charged Brother Bainbridge. However, the reptilian giant was ready. Once Diamond was in range, reality distorted around her, and iron chains appeared, then pinned her to the adjacent wall.

Giselle grinned smugly. However, before she could make it to her husband, Diamond loosened her binds just enough for her to sling the broken lantern stick. The javelin sliced through the air and Giselle's chest. A screech cut into the night. The heavy strike pinned Giselle to the ground.

Heavy rain stirred from the sky as the wind speed accelerated. Potted plants flew across the room as torches ripped from the walls. Large bees were swept up in the cyclone, and Bainbridge could hardly remain focused. Typhon laughed maniacally while the gusts emptied the pool water. Lightning broke from the clouds and hit the ground haphazardly.

Typhon glanced back at Giselle and winked. The water was electric. All of Bainbridge's alien men shuddered and fell as Typhon's gums peeled back, and his chuckle grew louder and more obnoxious. As the water touched Giselle's peach skin, her screech was earsplitting and echoed through the halls.

Focused, Bainbridge slowly pushed his palm forward. Massive fiery energy took Typhon off his feet and burnt half his body. The raven-haired mistress wiggled from her chains. She pried the lantern stick from Giselle's chest and lifted it above her head; however, before she could strike, the entire room lit up with artificial lighting.

"Freeze!"

Wide-eyed, Diamond dropped her weapon as Rhion Galloway entered the room with a team full of armed police officers. Typhon's storm slowly fizzled, and Bainbridge dropped his pink shield of psychic light. Confused and unsure of their next move, the four exchanged glances.

"What the fuck is going on here?" Rhion bellowed as Martin followed behind him.

"This shit isn't normal, man!" Martin cried with his gun raised. "We have to call for backup!"

Giselle stood from the ground, and water dripped from her wet clothing. After a moment, she nodded, and with an incredible amount of concentration, her voice dropped several octaves as she spoke to the crowd, "*Leave now. Forget everything you saw.*"

Like hypnotized army men, each police officer lowered their weapon and slowly marched out of the spa. Giselle began to cough. This spell was too much for her; she began to faint as she spit up blood. In a single gust of wind,

Typhon flew across the room, snatched Giselle by the waist, and shot through the open roof like a bat.

"What was that?" Diamond growled toward Brother Bainbridge, who now stood his standard 5'9 height. "You have to get better friends."

"Nothing!" Jormun Gandr swung his arms about as he shouted in the still raining parking lot. One after the other, the seven silent surrounding officers placed their pistols into their pockets. No one had ever seen Gandr so angry. As red and bloated as a tomato, he had a voice that was an explosion in the midnight parking lot, "You dragged us here and basically forced us to break into an empty spa, and for what?"

"I-I'm sorry," Rhion shook his head in disbelief and tried to speak, "I thought that…"

"That was full of 'killers and murders!'" Gandr quoted Rhion sarcastically. "What the actual fuck? What even gave you that stupid idea?"

"It was an anonymous tip," Rhion struggled for words, then looked over to Martin, who helplessly turned his face.

"An anonymous tip," annoyance ringed in his voice. Gandr nodded and bit his lower lips so hard it almost bled. He turned on his heel and began to stomp toward his car. "We came here because we trusted you! I put my job on the line for this. We all did! I will be reporting this…"

Chapter 19: Will Anyone Ever Understand Me?

"You shall not eat anything that has died naturally. You may give it to the sojourner who is within your towns, that he may eat it, or you may sell it to a foreigner. For you are a people holy to the Lord your God. You shall not boil a young goat in its mother's milk."
Deuteronomy 14:21

After a few hours of clean-up, Brother Bainbridge sat back on his throne by the pool. He was three times his normal size, and his eyes and teeth were shaded a yellow-green. Bainbridge's ritual had commenced. Rodent-size bees crawled from the naked flaps of skin. Blood poured from his wrist like wine, and the small gray men beneath him brawled for drops like hatchings fought for their mother's regurgitations. As the most powerful psychic in the quarter, Brother Bainbridge needed a few security officers. After all, Tristan was everywhere.

The King of Flies filled his lungs with the fresh scent of palm leaves covered in sulfur as Diamond washed his feet in the curved pool. Smaller skinless demons washed his hair with oil, and the monster nurses poured a greasy perfume on his naked chest. Bainbridge closed his eyes; the draining of his blood relaxed him.

An itch scratched at his temples. His psychic waves stretched way beyond his flesh. He could tell they approached. Annoyed that his ritual had been interrupted twice tonight, Bainbridge cracked a friendly smile.

Nathaniel Robinson and his wife Fran Miller Robinson entered the chamber with a much different attitude than Typhon and Giselle. Nathaniel and Fran had a peculiar marriage; they never touched, and Fran never spoke. As the daughter of Giselle and Nathaniel, she crafted precisely how he needed her to be, robust, silent, and, most of all—loyal.

Bainbridge carelessly focused his gaze on the two as if two salesmen had just interrupted his dinner. He began, "My home is popular tonight. Hello Nathaniel. Madam Fran."

"Let's cut pleasantries," Nathaniel was quick to interrupt when he pressed his feet in the ground as Fran crossed her fingers behind her back. "I know you got my message; Typhon and Lilith aren't exactly the most subtle."

"They don't know how to fight either," Diamond chuckled as she licked her lips.

"Human…" Nathaniel frowned when he addressed her, "you're out of your league."

"Not that I don't welcome a visit from an old buddy, but tell me why exactly you're here," Bainbridge asked, his smile buried beneath his annoyance.

"I know you have the Horseman," Nathaniel began. "I know you're working for the Hidden Eye. And I know they're going to betray you."

"And how would you know that…?" Bainbridge snickered.

"I have my ways," Nathaniel refused to admit and shrugged. "Hades doesn't just want a seat at the table; he wants your seat. Prepare yourself. It turns out he doesn't like leaving and loose ends unsnapped…"

"My own brothers! I-I don't believe you!" Bainbridge recoiled and cringed in disgust.

"You're a psychic," Nathaniel reminded the man in the sweater. "But you don't always know what to look for. Hades planted a failsafe inside of Uriel."

Bainbridge's lips thinned into a straight line. His third-eye circled Ezekiel's chamber. The boy sat on his fingertips as he sweated in agony. Bainbridge touched Ezekiel's mind, and instantly flashes of chaos crashed in like shattered glass. It tasted like offal. Pale and sickly. It was the taste of death.

"Mors," Bainbridge muttered the Horseman's name in disbelief.

It was a memory he could never forget. During the Great Fall, seraphim crashed from the Heavens like shooting stars. Pain choked him. The burning was something he had never felt before. As a smoldering hydrogen gas, he knew he had to take form. Steam wavered off the asteroid, and Bainbridge crafted his own human limbs.

This was a devolution. Once a presence made of detonating light and potentially poisonous otherworldly gas, he knew that he could not show his true form on Earth. He was delirious. Limited. His senses kicked in one after another.

He pressed his toes into the warm wet soil beneath him and looked toward the sky. Thousands of asteroids pelted toward Earth. Pretty soon, he was going to be among good company.

"Brother!"

Bainbridge was tackled to the ground as an explosion detonated just inches away from him. Before Bainbridge could even see straight, he was getting dragged away. Fire chased him, and the very ground shook.

Once they stopped running, Bainbridge dropped to the ground. The descent was a polarizing experience, and when his vision cleared, there he saw Walt Excel. He was a middle-aged man with frizzy white hair around his ears and the back of his neck. Five other humanoid spirits surrounded Walt. They spoke in Enochian and Walt was the first to address him.

"It's a war zone out there," he concluded. "Everybody's fighting for power. They were going to eat you up."

"I-I" Bainbridge was shaking and could hardly speak.

"You see, they try to get you right after you fall so that you're too weak to defend yourself. It takes some adjusting, but you'll get through it." Walt was encouraging.

"W-w-who are you?" Bainbridge cringed when he spoke. "Everything hurts! I cannot smell in this form!"

"I am Mammon," he grunted. "Earth has limited resources. Everybody's fighting over them, and I don't want to share. I warrant the seven of us stick together. We'll run this planet in no time. We'll be like family…. What did you say your name was?"

"Beelzebub…" Bainbridge murmured. He was still delirious, but he was sure. Bainbridge took Walt's hand and finally felt like he belonged.

How could his brothers betray him?

How could they let Hades take his place in the Hidden Eye? No. He refused to be replaced.

"I have the information you want. Maybe we can work out a deal?" Nathaniel tilted his head and smirked.

"How do I know if I can trust you?" Bainbridge questioned and raised a brow.

"Do you really think I would tell you that?" Nathaniel scoffed and took a step forward. "Bestow the Horsemen onto me or kill them immediately. I know of them. Kill them now, or you'll regret it."

"You underestimate me yet again," Bainbridge frowned.

"But Mom," Cody, the red-headed twenty-eight year old protested as his mother snatched a cup of coffee off the table. Willie and Marshall shot Cody sorry glances, and Cody cleared his throat. "I'm an adult man! We agreed I can have one cup of coffee!"

"Decaf or hot chocolate only!" Sylvia Goldenblatt implored, then pressed the giant coffee cup to her wrinkled pink lips and, within seconds, devoured the entire serving. She took a deep breath and adjusted her tortoise turtle shell glasses with her chubby little finger. Her bold voice shouted above all others in the Mermaid Cafe, "Cody, you know caffeine makes you nervous!"

"Well, maybe I wouldn't be so nervous if you didn't keep me up all night!" he snarled. The four-eyed redhead itched at his baby blue sweater that covered his white polyester shirt and dark orange tie. "And your sweater itches like heck!"

"Watch your mouth!" Sylvia threatened, then crushed the paper cup in her hands and tossed it into a nearby trash can. "It's just in case someone wants to offer you a job. You have to look presentable."

She twirled a finger around her large beaded green necklace then buried her fists into her overlapping love-handles before she reminded him, "You know, the Cohens' son has already been offered four jobs since college! But no, not my son! All my son wants to do is look at Chinese pornography!"

Cody's fists dropped to his sides as his red glasses nearly fell off his blushing freckled face. He was blood boiled. His mother controlled every aspect of his life. She was judgmental but always wrong. Cody gritted his teeth and shouted, "It's not pornography; it's Anime!"

"So they say," Sylvia sneered, then turned on her heel. "So how long do you boys need? When should I come by to pick you up?"

"We'll be alright, Ms. Goldenblatt," Willie shivered.

"We'll call you if we need a ride," Marshall confirmed. Sylvia made eye contact with her son and silently warned him about drinking coffee before exiting the small shop.

Annoyed and ashamed, Marshall leaned in a little closer to his colleagues. "Okay, Cody, why are we here?"

"You're not going to believe this," Cody prefaced his story, "but a couple of days ago, an owl came to my window. I couldn't tell if I was dreaming or not, but it screamed 'Mermaid Cafe.' So I've been going to every Mermaid Cafe in the city and look who works at this one..."

Cody nudged towards a young tan girl who battled with the steamed espresso machine and over-boiled milk. The brunette blew her long thick curls from her face and popped her gum as she shot a co-worker a grimace.

"I told you I didn't know how to do it!" Clara Rodriguez hissed at her co-worker.

"You mean to tell me we came back here because you wanted to stalk that girl?" Marshall accused him while he had smoke coming out of his ears. With a sneer, he kicked backward, "We agreed if you wanted camera time, you had to bring us a big lead!"

"Yeah," Willie agreed. "And she doesn't like you anyway."

"That's not why we're here!" Cody stuttered and scrambled for his knapsack. "The readings here have been off the charts; I think this may be another hot spot." He unzipped his bag and stopped mid-swipe to ask, "How do you know she doesn't like me?"

"You guys talking about me?" Clara revealed herself, folded her arms, cocked her hips, and stomped her feet all at once.

"N-no," Cody stuttered.

"I saw your mom yell at you. Aren't you a little old to be drinking hot chocolate?" she asked. Clara slanted her eyes as her memory removed doubt, "Hey, aren't you those fake reporters who tried to talk to me after that thing happened with the kids?"

"I think you'd remember," Marshall whispered to himself. "Since when do you work here?"

"I have a few jobs," Clara replied matter-of-factly. "You think that one little teaching gig could support me and Tití?"

"Duh? No," she answered her own question then continued on her stream of thought. "Ain't nobody gonna pay Tití's hospital bills but me. Why are you guys here, anyways?"

"We," Cody hesitantly took the floor, "we were worried about you. Sometimes when people have traumatic experiences, they tend to suffer from PTS."

Clara lifted a perplexed eyebrow and spat in disgust, "Ew, first of all, that's none of your business, and second of all, no, my time of the month isn't until next week, and third of all, I'm from the Bronx—you don't have to worry about me."

"We just wanted to see if you were safe," Cody cleared his throat before he answered. "Has anything weird happened to you? I mean… since the incident?"

"No," Clara admitted, then shook her head in bewilderment, "Well, I got this new job…and I don't know what, but they keep giving me stuff to do…"

"Anything else?" Cody pushed further.

"Besides that, sometimes I do get a weird feeling around this place when it gets dark. Like someone is watching me or something," Clara admitted, "then there's like a lost bird that gets stuck in here and screams. Sometimes it sounds like words. I don't know."

"An owl?" Willie suddenly seemed interested as his words sparked with excitement. "What would it say?"

"I don't know some kind of bird. It would be like 'Bible talk,' you know?" Clara answered but was finally annoyed with the conversation. "Listen, if you want to come by after I lock up, you could stay and see for yourself. It's here, like, every day."

"Cody, you did get a reading on that doohickey," Marshall confirmed before he looked at Clara. "You'll just let us camp out here and film?"

"For fifty bucks," Clara declared and began to tap her foot impatiently. "Ay Dios Mío, listen, I have to get back to work. I don't care what you do, but I'm still new, I don't wanna get in trouble so I will deny everything. I'll leave the back open tonight. Just don't forget the fifty bucks!"

Chapter 20: The Great Escape

"See what kind of love the Father has given to us, that we should be called children of God; and so we are. The reason why the world does not know us is that it did not know him. Beloved, we are God's children now, and what we will be has not yet appeared; but we know that when he appears we shall be like him, because we shall see him as he is."

John 3:1-2

"Neil!" she chanted his name so many times, it gave her a headache. Her throat itched with a parched heat that made her cough. Typically, Neil would immediately answer. The veins in Aurora's eyes were so angry and swollen that her tears dried before they dropped from her ducts.

Frustrated and disappointed, Aurora slammed her fist into the wall. She knew he was in the cell beside her. She knew he could hear her call. Aurora's mouth gaped as she dry heaved silently. How could he? She trusted him.

Neil wobbled his head to clear Aurora's echoing call. The angel knew she was in no physical danger, and even if she was, there was nothing he could do to help. He was right where he needed to be. Diamond chewed on the long red nails that extended from her left hand. The Seal of Solomon curled around her shiny black hair extensions.

Diamond was wearing a leather tube top that was more expensive than it appeared. Her lipstick was a greasy red, and her pale cheeks were blushed with a rosy shadow; the ex-stripper seemed to be prepared for this encounter. Diamond leaned back on her ivory bathtub and winked at the naked angel.

"I finally figured you out," Neil announced as Aurora's voice faded into oblivion. "Why you've been calling me here every night. Why you like me so much."

"Oh?" she asked. Diamond's nostrils flared as she folded her arms. "Just because you're in my mind, don't think you know me! Thought I told you about that."

"Don't flatter yourself," Neil chuckled. "It doesn't take Sigmund Freud to see that you're into me because of my power. You turned down these lights so you could get a taste. I'm the most powerful angel in the world, and you like to be dominated."

"Dominated?" Diamond wrinkled her nose and snarled in anger. "You angels got some real big egos, huh?"

Like a snake in ecstasy, she slinked off her Jacuzzi-sized tub and slithered toward Neil. A coy smirk bent the edges of her lips as she slid a long red fingernail under Neil's chin as she whispered, "You are the most powerful angel in the world, but I like you because I dominate you!"

Diamond launched a substantial blow to Neil's gut, and before he could hit the ground, she lifted him by the thick hairs on his head. She spat in his face and tossed him aside like a pound of fertilizer. Before Neil could regain his composure, Diamond mounted him.

She pressed her silver ring into his forehead so hard it left an imprint on his physical body. She threatened, "All my life, I've been dominated. Even my older brother just took what he wanted from me. But look at you. Everybody's afraid of you. And you're my boy toy. Finally, I get to take what I want."

It was just as she had foreseen. Neil had ignored her call. He had chosen another woman. Aurora's rabbit-like eyes were dark with hues of red. The fabric of time was hers to weave, sow, and cut, but she had never felt so debilitated. She could feel that the intensity of the energy-sucking fluorescent lights waned, and her strength though not fully saturated rose with every moment. Visions of past and future revealed themselves in fractured, inconsistent clips; however, now she could also see the present.

Her sight was blurred, but there he stood. Diamond was in her luxurious chamber, and Neil was in her mind. Without a stitch of clothing, he plowed himself into Diamond Love as she yanked at his thick chestnut hair and yelped seductively.

At first, Aurora could only view their intercourse through fragmented flashes, but she tasted it as she grew stronger. She could smell the salty, pungent aroma of sex. Aurora could feel when Diamond scratched Neil's back and could hear her scream out with pleasure.

Aurora's skin quivered, and her eyes filled with stubborn tears. She could see the smile on Neil's face and sense the shared enjoyment between him and his lover. Desperate, disgusted, and tired, Aurora folded her legs and concentrated on present times.

Her eyes returned to their standard color as a knock sounded at her door. Brother Bainbridge was surrounded by bees and the two gray monsters, "Hello Gabriel."

Diamond was distracted by Neil's penis.

Bainbridge was alone.

It was now or never.

Slowly, Aurora breathed in through her nose and freed the air through her puckered lips. Invisible energy popped off her like hot grease from a frying pan. Though she did not feel ready, she knew she only had one shot. Bainbridge was powerful, and as he approached, Aurora struggled to remain focused. She gritted her teeth and wrinkled her nose.

"Hello, bitch," Aurora miffed and unleashed. Glowing smoke paralyzed all things that moved. Tints of gray shadowed Aurora's fifteen-foot range like a black and white movie in extreme slow motion.

Bainbridge was unlike any demon she had ever frozen. Aurora could feel him fight through her power, and she had no idea how long her spell would last. Her eyes were large and red, but she was like a fawn who walked for the first time, confused and unsure. She had seen the future and knew that in her plan, she would never escape. However, there was still hope.

Neil showed little resistance as Diamond pressed him on the cool tile floor. He was the most powerful being he knew, but he had to admit a part of him liked to be controlled. The raven-haired seductress desperately scratched at his neck before she moved her right hand down to his chest and perky nipples.

He was entirely under her guide. With the unapologetic touch of her fingers, she rushed the blood from his heart down his body. Diamond pressed herself into him. She could tell that he needed little convincing as she encouraged his body to throb in her hands.

"Ezekiel!" Aurora called out so loudly that her voice cracked. "I froze him! The lights are low! I have to stay here, but I don't know how long I can hold this son of a bitch!" She gulped. "Get Amanda, she's the only one who can escape!"

Ezekiel pressed a hand against the glass in his cell. He failed to see Aurora or what she was going through, but her words were loud and clear. Without thinking, Ezekiel placed his full trust in her. The angel lowered his head, and within milliseconds astral projected into Amanda's holding cell.

Aurora was right; his powers were returning.

"Amanda!" Ezekiel struggled to speak through slight feverishness. "I don't know what's going on, but now's the time to get the hell out."

"How?" Amanda asked and quirked an eyebrow. "What about the lights?"

"Screw the lights!" Ezekiel shouted with the same intensity Aurora rushed upon him. "You're fine! Aurora said you're the only one who can escape! You're our only hope; it's time to go off! Take no prisoners! Get out as fast as you can and get to Lyssah!"

Amanda's eyes immediately teared up, but she dared not argue with Ezekiel when he was this sure. She wrapped her white towel tighter around her body, and unassured, she muttered, "Okay…"

The blonde angel placed a flat palm on the glass door that imprisoned her, and in seconds it shattered. Ezekiel was right. She felt more powerful than she had in days.

She placed her foot outside her cell, and there Aurora was. Bainbridge and two of his minions were slowed in the white smoke. Aurora's fingers were arched, and her eyes were scarlet. As a droplet of blood dripped from her nostrils, Aurora turned to Amanda, who stood there in awe.

"Go!"

"I-I don't want to leave you!" Amanda cried, her shoulders sunk, and her face grew rosy with alarm. "I can't!"

Aurora looked directly at her. Amanda had never heard Aurora so angry. The time-witch gritted through her teeth, "I've seen the future! I have to hold him here! Go, hurry!"

Ezekiel's spirit appeared before Amanda. He had surveyed the area. Readily he informed her, "We're two floors down. The staircase is the last door to the right!"

Unable to think, Amanda just kowtowed to Aurora's command. The blonde took off in a sprint towards the staircase. Despair and panic overwhelmed her as her eyes welled with water.

She swung open the hefty metal door and entered the emergency concrete staircase. Heaves of sorrow battled with

Amanda's mind, and tears ran down her face like water through a sprinkler. How could she leave Aurora, Neil, and Ezekiel behind? In her path stood three men who all looked exactly the same. The triplets wore white vests and black skinny tuxedo pants. Their movements were effeminate and synchronized as they flipped their perfectly styled black hair and placed their hands on their hips.

"Are you lost, ma'am?" the first one asked.

"May we escort you back to your room?" the second continued.

"Or get you a nice, warm," the third Tristan narrowed his eyes and finished, "towelette?"

Amanda almost answered their questions, but after a moment, she knew these men were evil. With a substantial exhale, Amanda transformed herself into an animal she knew very well. Steam rose from her, and as a mallard, she took to the air.

Each man grabbed at her, and though her flying skills were subpar, she was able to avoid their grasp. As a human, she swung open the door and entered the lobby. Her jaw dropped. Exquisite and expensive, the lobby was a massive vestibule of luxury. However, she hardly had time to take in the beautiful scenery.

Ezekiel appeared before her in a ghostly glow and commanded, "Hurry! The exit is around the corner. It's locked; you have to break it down."

Amanda tightened her towel and bit her lower lip as hot tears streamed down her face. Barefoot, she made a run toward to exit; however, out of the shadows, Tristan appeared in six identical bodies.

"Ma'am," the closest Tristan spoke first. His words were always polite but always saturated with sass, "The cathedral is closed for the evening."

"Allow me to escort you back to your room," the second Tristan spoke.

"There, we can make sure you're very comfortable," a third voice warned.

"Now, please, this way," the fourth Tristan cocked his neck like a snake and folded his arms.

"Kill them!" Ezekiel's spirit materialized before the angel in a state of trepidation as he yelled.

The blonde angel fell into autopilot. She stomped a barefoot onto the white tiles beneath her and arched her fingers in an aggressive assault. The Tristan closest to her bursted in a fit of flames.

Amanda took off into a dash; however, she only made it a few feet before one of the Tristans took her into his arms. A second clone clocked her in the face. Then a third trapped her in a headlock.

Amanda yelped out in agony. She hated her power because she could never remember anything; however, something came to her mind. Her training with Lyssah. The periodic table of elements was confusing and extensive. Yet, at this stressful time, she did remember bits of it. Marble… $CaCO_3$… contained….clay, micas, quartz, pyrite, iron oxides, and graphite.

Amanda's palms grew a bright white light, and within seconds the men who attacked her were steaming frozen statues. She pushed them to the ground, and as they shattered, the third Tristan sucker-punched her in the nose three times.

Blood burst from the blonde blunderbuss's broken nostrils. Instinctually Amanda waved a palm, and Tristan dropped to his knees. He mewled like an animal as redness fizzed out of his eyes, nose, mouth, and ears. Tristan weaved and waned. Instantly, his blood became hydrochloric acid and leaked from his body, then ate at the tile below.

Astonished, Amanda impressed herself, but more men stood before her exit. In her state of confusion, she could not tell how many Tristan clones were in the darkroom; she made it only a few steps before three more men jumped before her.

Already weak and exhausted Amanda raised her fists, but before anyone could strike, Ezekiel appeared. He was surrounded by tadpole-like ectoplasmic creatures that moved around like wayward spirits. With a thrust of his wrists, the ghosts attacked the three men and stunned them.

"Keep going!" Ezekiel yelled.

Tears streamed from Amanda's eyes like water from a broken dam. She rushed past Ezekiel's projection and made it around the hallway. Before she made it around the corner, another four Tristans stood.

"How many of your people are there?" Amanda questioned in a desperate wail.

"You're never going to make it," the first Tristan cocked an eyebrow as he spoke.

Amanda pressed towards the nearest object in her reach. A rack of warm towels. With a cloth in hand, Amanda swung with all of her strength. Obsidian was hard and brittle with very sharp edges. It was a naturally occurring volcanic glass. Amanda recalled: SiO_2; silicon dioxide. The fabric morphed into a slick and acute black material. Amanda waved the weapon relentlessly.

With the first desperate swipe, Amanda was able to slit a throat. Hot blood popped onto her face like boiling oil from a frying pan. With the second swing, she cut another Tristan's face and sent him to the floor. Her third strike contacted the man's eye. Amanda tried to escape, but the clones grabbed at her feet.

Iron.

Within seconds the obsidian blade transformed into a generic iron baseball bat. It took all of her energy, but Amanda bashed in the head of the clone that grabbed at her feet, demolishing his skull and brains into chopped cabbage. The front door was in her vision. She made a desperate lap toward the exit, but of course, three Tristan clones blocked her escape.

"Stay a little longer," the first one spat.

"You need a facial," the second continued.

In the blink of an eye, the entire room was filled with short-haired, small-framed young men. Like the cells of an organism, each identical being besieged her with a singular unified objective. Amanda lifted her baseball bat but was assaulted mid-swing.

Tristan's physical strength was at most twice as strong as any man's, but Amanda had been hit with much harder. Responsively, Amanda clocked the teeth out of one of the brown-haired men. His mouth shattered as spit and blood splattered across her face. She went in for another strike but was met with a knife in her shoulder.

Her white towel absorbed her blood like a parasite. She fell to her knees and was kicked in the face and thrown in another headlock. There were so many clones that Amanda had no idea which direction they attacked. The angel was taken from every side. Amanda shut her eyes as tightly as possible and took in a deep breath.

NaCl, salt.

Crystallized, the men around her dropped like fallen cherry snow cones. Horrified at her own power, she watched as their salty skins melted in pools of their own blood. There was a time in Amanda's life where she declared herself a pacifist. Now, the very idea was so distant from her mind. She was a murderer. Period.

"Just let us go, okay?" Amanda cried as a hot tear rushed down her face.

Her wide blue eyes dropped so much water her cheeks were brackish. Weakly Amanda tossed the metal baseball bat to the ground. Her fingers fisted. Steam rose off her, and her shape changed. Within moments she was shorter, hairier, and more muscular.

As a chimpanzee, Amanda took to the air. In seconds she bodied the first Tristan and took his face apart with only a few swipes. As the other two moved toward her, she leaped across the cash register, but her newfound animal instinct and agility failed as she crashed to the ground.

Opposable toes. She had forgotten chimps had those. As her appendages wailed, Tristan appeared before her with a standing candelabra in his hands. Amanda tried to move, but he shoved the razor end through her shoulder.

Amanda released an animalistic cry that echoed throughout the entire building. Clones piled on top of her. She considered burning down the whole building, but the fact that her friends still resided within ceased her thirst for destruction. Multiple Tristans took hold of the ape as she fizzled back into a blonde.

Aurora's spell dwindled. The fog around Bainbridge and his minions faded. Weakly, Aurora stumbled to the ground. She wiped the blood from her nostrils.

"Nice try," Brother Bainbridge clapped as he floated toward her. "You can have an A for your effort."

"Or," Aurora sniffled, "you can take this effort up your A."

Aurora dashed to the burning torches on the walls. Amanda was not willing to burn this place to the ground, but Aurora was. With militant accuracy, the angel tossed the first torch directly into Bainbridge's face.

Her power was not at full force, and instead of freezing her enemies completely, she was only able to slow them for as long as she could hold her breath. Desperately, she tossed the next torch she could find to the ground. Aurora rushed toward the staircase.

Before she reached the door, however, Bainbridge manifested before her in a wiggle of reality. Unharmed and with a smile, he lifted a palm.

Aurora's eyes lit up with a red light, but Bainbridge made a fist before she was able to summon her full ability. A crushing force surrounded Aurora. Her body crumpled as easily as paper. She was lifted from the ground and moved with an excessive speed. Aurora was pelted into her cell like a baseball hit by a professional player. The glass doors slammed and locked behind her.

Brother Bainbridge appeared in Diamond's chambers. As a talented psychic, he was able to view Neil as he mentally had intercourse with his most trusted advisor. By a simple finger wave, Bainbridge telekinetically separated the lovers. He pinned Neil against the wall and stepped into the room with a fit of authoritative but almost passive anger.

"Miss Love," Bainbridge questioned. "What on earth are you doing?"

In a state of shock, Diamond covered herself with a towel before she answered, "These are toys, right? I was just playing with them!"

"Behind my back," Bainbridge huffed. "I expected more from you."

"It wasn't behind your back," Diamond defended herself. "But what the hell? Do I have to tell you about everything I do?"

"Yes!" Bainbridge's fingers expanded, and suddenly Neil was returned to his cell. Bainbridge stepped closer to Diamond and whispered, "I'm sorry, my dear, but now you must be punished…"

Diamond attempted to respond but found herself in new surroundings. First, she could hear nothing but a howling echo. She tried to move but was chained to a rocky wall in a volcanic mouth. She hung above a pit of burning stones as snakes hissed around her. Though she scrambled, she was unable to escape the iron binds. Raging steam smelled like rotten eggs, and giant rattlesnakes moved with a unified and demonic intention.

Diamond screamed as loud as she could as the animals roughly forced themselves underneath her towel and into her private areas. They entered her ultimately, sank their fangs into her flesh, and violated her body. The raven-haired warrior wailed out in pain but was powerless to stop their sexual invasion.

Chapter 21: Fire Ring 9: The List of Victims

"But the day of the Lord will come like a thief, and then the heavens will pass away with a roar, and the heavenly bodies will be burned up and dissolved, and the earth and the works that are done on it will be exposed."
Peter 3:10

"Welcome to another beautiful day, my friends! How did we enjoy our Hot Yoga revitalization? I know we tried to leave our lovely spa, and I'm sorry you had to go through this, but now I hope we know those efforts are futile." Bainbridge's smile was warmer than ever when he spoke. "Not until treatment is over. This is better, isn't it? Submit. You angels are weak, and I can crush you with a thought. We have dug deep, haven't we?" Brother Bainbridge tightened the restraints around Amanda's wrists. Chained to the walls, the fallen angels sweat until their flesh was red and moist. They had been there for a week.

Punished for their attempted escape, the four were locked in distorted positions by the demon who danced around an increasingly growing flame in the center of the room.

Amanda's wide blue eyes woefully glanced over to her colleagues as they cooked like hamburgers on a grill. She was in agony, and the demon did not stop inducing her most painful memories.

"However, there is still some digging we must do. Tradition dictates I need to rip out your innards, with love, of course. For the love of Brother Bainbridge. This is your final treatment and the cure to your addiction: The Last Fire Ring. Open your heart unto me, and I shall cleanse you! I have brought you some tonic before your treatment."

"Instead of a Fire Ring, think we can do a cool refreshing Water Ring instead?" Ezekiel murmured sarcastically.

"More blood?" Sweat dripped into Amanda's eyes as she growled at the man in the sweater. "Please! You keep saying we're friends, but friends don't do this to each other!"

"You've had us drinking your Kool-Aid for a while now," Neil uttered suspiciously, "I'm starting to get sick of it."

Diamond Love's eyes locked with Neil's, but she had nothing to say. Pissed and embarrassed, she folded her arms beneath her large breasts.

"Branch out," Aurora chimed in, catching the general theme of joking in the face of danger, "maybe come out with a diet version? Blood Lite?"

"What's the plan, Brother Bainbridge?" Neil asked with his voice deep, "You've been at it for weeks now. If you wanted us dead. You would have killed us already. You can't be doing this just for kicks!"

"Oh, come now, I do not need to answer you," Brother Bainbridge announced, then floated to Aurora. "Now, this spa has a multitude of services. I think you will enjoy it! You little bitch, I know you were behind the escape plan. Now, let's get your nails all pretty."

With the help of Diamond Love, Brother Bainbridge forced Aurora out of her shackles and back into prison. Though she struggled, her attempts were no match against the two. The angel, however, had been saving her strength all day. With a blast of red light, an energy flew from her eyes and shadowed everything she saw in black and white tints.

Aurora panted frailty as a droplet of blood crawled from her nostril. Fear gripped her spine, and she wanted to run, as she never knew how long she could keep her enemies in-between dimensions, but as per her vision, she had to follow her plan.

Beside her massage table, a small gray creature carried a pair of sharp pliers to which she quickly snatched. In the center of Diamond's ivory forehead, Aurora carved the symbol of an ankh.

"Bitch!" she yelled as the angel's spell burst, and Aurora kicked her to the wooden planks on the floor. Aurora rushed toward the exit as Bainbridge snatched her up like a mother cat would a kitten.

"What a naughty little girl," Bainbridge exhaled in disappointment when Aurora spat in his face.

"That little cunt cut me!" Diamond shouted and tended to the new bleeding scar on her forehead.

"You'll heal," Brother Bainbridge snarled. "Now, help me put the child to bed."

The Z'New strapped the angel to the massage table, and Brother Bainbridge prepared as his smaller gray demons handed him a pair of pliers.

Aurora breathed heavily and braced her body for whatever he was about to do. His treatments were strange, and she never knew his plans. She did know, however, that it would hurt.

Aurora shut her eyes and warned, "If you fucking touch me again, I swear to God I'm going to come for you. I don't need to see into the future to know that when I escape from here, I'm going to make your little Hell Spa look like a Black Friday at Neiman Marcus with only *a single pair* of Louboutin, red sole platforms left *but* maybe less bloody."

"Stop it; she's serious!" Amanda blurted a cautious warning.

Brother Bainbridge let out a hearty bellow, "We are feeling spirited today! We're just here to get your nails done! We'll cure your addiction in no time. No more human soul. No more bodily anchors. You'll be at your full potential! You'll finally be able to do whatever you want to do! Free."

"Let me out of these restraints, and I'll show you what I want to do," Aurora threatened through gritting her teeth.

"In time, you will see that I am right." Brother Bainbridge grabbed Aurora's right foot and held it in his hand for a moment before he spoke again. "I think a nice pedicure-manicure is in order."

With blurring agility, the demon pinched the toenail on Aurora's big toe between the pliers and, in one swift motion, tore it right off. Aurora's yelp echoed through the spa hallways as she almost passed out in torment.

14 Years Ago

Everyone knew that Brita Ahman High School dances were a minimal effort put together by lazy teachers who only participated because they were required. Because the air conditioning was too high, the gym was a steam room full of sweat and prepubescent gases. The cheap red and blue paper decorations represented the school's colors and had been recycled for years. Due to the lack of budget, there was no catering or food service save the lonely bowl of potato chips beside the cooler of mysterious red punch. The teachers found time to blow up six blue balloons before retreating on their cigarette breaks, allowing the Christian DJ to supervise the apathetic crowd.

The worst part about it was the lack of mature men.

Aurora and her friends escaped immediately since they had other Valentine's Day plans.

Ivanna was invited to a college house party, which meant Aurora and Sasha were about to have the time of their lives.

Dank and merciless undercurrent suffocated the girls like a molded wet blanket. The frat house was filled with fetid, rank bodies that jumped to the beat of the loud rock music and added scents to the air so putrid that it made Aurora's eyes water. Her senses felt attacked, the music was deafening, her nose wrinkled instinctually at the marijuana smoke, her eyesight burnt with cigar residue, and she could taste the vomit in her mouth as she forced it back down her throat.

It took her a moment, but Aurora never thought the smell of beer and sweat could excite her the way it did. At first, the roaring music and rowdy boys overwhelmed them. However, as their hearts pounded while adrenaline kicked in, they slowly felt the uninhibited opportunities that came with being a young adult. She and her crew had never attended a college function; this is what freedom felt like. The two-story house was filled with enough perspiring college students to overflow a volleyball court. Three mischievous grins lined the faces of the high school girls.

"Ladies," Ivanna hesitantly shifted her custom-made designer purse over her shoulder when she whispered. "We stick out like three sore thumbs…"

Gray eye-shadow, thick cover-up, and peach lip gloss caked Aurora's face like a new layer of leathery skin as she nervously observed the room. Ivanna was right. Every girl that was at the party was in jeans and t-shirts. Aurora was loaded into a red and orange skirt that was two-sizes under her weight, and her breasts were pinned in so tightly that if she sneezed, she would bust a stitch. Her glossy extensions reached down to her buttock, and her three-inch beige heels made her several inches taller. Ivanna's outfit wasn't much different as her skirt was leather designed like a rainbow and reached just below her crotch.

The posse was dressed like they were about to go to an S&M-themed prom. Sasha suddenly felt like they made a mistake with tight skirts, perfectly pressed hair, and lips greasier than a corrupt politician. She whined in shame, "We look like whores!"

"Don't be a chicken shit," Aurora taunted discourteously. "Ivanna was invited to this party, and she invited us. We have every right to be here. And who cares if we stick out? Isn't that a good thing? We look good. I would hate to be on the same level as these full-bodied lumberjacks they call women."

The girls erupted in a fit of laughter.

Sasha reapplied her lipstick and agreed, "You are funny, Aurora, and so right!"

Aurora confidently placed her hands on her hips and absorbed the praise like daybreak on a happy sunflower. She was empowered and led the crew to the punch bowl, which was filled with something the college kids referred to as "Jungle Juice." It tasted like metal and was almost painful to get down, but the girls followed suit as they filled their red cups and made scrunchy faces as they drank.

After a few songs, selfies, social media posts, and refills, the party had grown wilder. As the dance turned into screams, then to shoves and bumps, Aurora was nearly thrown to the ground. Her eyes burned red as she wiped her spilled drink from her dress.

She had seen this brawny sophomore get louder the more he drank. Stocky and short, his shaggy hair looked as though it were cut with a butter knife, he smelt like rotten fruit, and his lips had a distortive curve. Instantly Aurora fixated on him with blind rage and barked, "Watch where you're going! You ugly frumpy ass troglodyte!"

"What?" the boy asked and raised an eyebrow. He grabbed his crotch and scoffed, "All man here, sweetie, nothing trans-whatever about me."

"I said 'troglodyte!' It's a fat nasty troll-like beast that no one wants to be around!" Aurora publicly shamed him. "You could have ruined my dress, you goddamn douche-bro."

"Cool it," Sasha nervously whispered to Aurora, "That's Gary Winestine's best friend… you know, the guy who threw this party!"

"I know the guy who threw this party!" Perry declared. "Don't be a bitch!"

"Yeah Aurora," Ivanna urged, "Don't be a bitch…"

"Uh," Aurora swallowed a rock in her throat. She was losing the support of her friends. Meekly, she lifted her shoulders and apologized, "Umm…You know? Now that I think about it, you are not quite as sweaty as a troglodyte… my mistake; it's just dark in here…"

"Are you sure?" he asked, almost swaying in his glazed-over expression.

"Yup," Aurora lied through her teeth, "you definitely missed the mark."

"You're lucky you're so cute; otherwise, I would have you thrown out of here," Perry drunkenly smirked. "Why don't you come and see the room I'm staying in?"

His stench was overpowering. Aurora retreated a step, but her friends placed their hands on her back and reinforced

her stance. Ivanna mumbled, "Come on, Aurora, he's…
kinda… cute."

"Please," Sasha begged, "you're gonna get us kicked
out!"

It was a cramped and dirty room with peeling paint
and old, deteriorated furniture. A basket of putrid laundry
carried a scent of spoiled produce, and even though it was
late, the loud music kept the flies abuzz. Perry threw his dirty
laundry and a bottle of massage oil off of his bed and onto
the ground to make room for Aurora. She apprehensively sat
as he flung his meaty arm around her.

"Relax… I'm okay. You like my room?" Perry spoke
as though he already knew the answer, "My father owns a car
dealership. I'm gonna work with him after I graduate. Make
all kinds of money. Inherit the business after he's gone. You
like money, right, baby?"

"Who doesn't?" Aurora acknowledged and shrugged
as she pulled away but was trapped by the sheer weight of his
arm.

"I'm just looking for a girl I can take with me,"
Perry's breath smelled rotten, and his eyes were only
half-open. He was drunk and dribble crept out the corners of
his lips, when he uttered, "Could be you."

He kissed her lips sloppily. Aurora's stomach ran up
in knots. The tiny hairs on her arms stood, and anxiety
paralyzed her body. Perry placed his hands underneath her
skirt then pulled at her white laced thong. Aurora's nostrils
were enlarged.

"Stop," she pressed and yanked his hand down as
they locked eyes. They were so close Aurora could feel his
hot breath radiating on her face. "I can't do this," Aurora
finally admitted, "I-I'm a virgin."

"I knew it," Perry sighed deeply. He placed his hands
over his face and repressed a chuckle that emerged as a grin.
"From the moment I saw you walk through those doors, you
looked so hot and so confused. You don't belong here. You
think you're hot shit; think you could speak to me anyway
you fucking any way you want? You're way too young to be
at a college party. Someone needed to teach you a lesson. I

told my buddy, 'That's the kind of girl that deserves to get raped.'"

Aurora rushed for the door but was quickly pinned to the twin bed by the overpowering man. Though she screamed, the blaring speakers conquered her. Perry placed his hand over her mouth and held her down with his body weight.

With his other hand, he rammed his fingers underneath her panties. She was tight and a real virgin. Using a skill that was granted only through practice, he speedily removed her skirt. She wrestled with his size, but what Perry lacked in height, he made up for with strength.

He refused to bother with protection; why would he need to with a virgin? Perry removed his dark blue jeans, then ravaged and invaded her. Aurora's legs clenched then trembled. She kicked at the air until her limbs fell like a shoelace. She was powerless to stop her aggressor. Hot tears ran down her eyes as her bleats were unheard. Her body was taken over.

Present Day

"I pledge myself to you," Aurora cried in her sleep, "Brother Bainbridge."

With a small echo, Aurora's last fingernail was dropped into a silver bucket. Blood dripped from her naked digits and puddled beneath her table. A coy grin graced his face as he sneered smugly. "Now, that's a girl! Good show! I knew a nail job was all you needed!"

Chapter 22: Fire Ring 10: Amends

"Under their wings on their four sides, they had human hands. And the four had their faces and their wings thus: their wings touched one another. Each one of them went straight forward, without turning as they went. As for the likeness of their faces, each had a human face. The four had the face of a lion on the right side, the four had the face of an ox on the left side, and the four had the face of an eagle. Such were their faces. And their wings were spread out above. Each creature had two wings, each of which touched the wing of another, while two covered their bodies."

Ezekiel 1:8-11

Aurora was exhausted, and her threshold for pain waned. Within moments she had passed out. Once Aurora had exhausted herself from screaming, Brother Bainbridge and his swarm of five-foot-tall gray men approached Amanda. Her lip quivered, but she hardly fought as they released her from her restraints. The angel was dragged to an area she had never seen before. It was bare and almost normal, except for the Jacuzzi that was built into the center of the room.

It was surprising, but the room was even hotter than the others. Her eyes rolled back into her head as the gray demons chained her inside of the bubbling pool. At first, she was numb to the touch of the hot water. Amanda was delirious, and it took her a moment, but once inside, she realized this was unlike any pool she had ever seen. Steam and blended organs boiled around her in the red water. Amanda gasped for air. Eyeballs and chunks of flesh spun around her body in foaming, bloody fizz.

"Your final treatment Amanda, your Fire Ring, is a deep soak," Brother Bainbridge announced and ran his fingers through her bloodstained blonde hair. He kissed her forehead and confirmed, "Relax, you're almost done."

11 Years ago

Once her period had ceased, everything changed. Amanda had a pebble in her throat. Like a tumor, it grew, and like a dam, it felt like it severed the connection between her brain and heart. Intellect and soul battled until neither had the vigor to continue. Numbness washed over her. Desensitized, deep down, she was left with a chalky emptiness that tasted incomplete and guilty.

"It's okay, baby," Bethany cooed as she wrapped her arms around Amanda. "Momma's here."

Most of the time, she firmly believed in her mother's direction. Bethany led a model life. She was married, active in the church, a great mother, and homemaker. Amanda wanted nothing but to follow in her mother's footsteps. However, this felt utterly wrong.

Bethany professed that her daughter betrayed God with her act of perversion, but when Amanda took the test, the blonde knew it was a blessing. The idea of having a child thrilled Amanda; she had always imagined herself a good parent. She wanted nothing more, but Bethany forbade it, shamed her, and assured her she wasn't ready.

A world of opportunity and adventure felt ripped from Amanda. Emma would have been her child's name if she had been a daughter, Andrew if he had been born male. She had already picked out clothes and designed the nursery in her mind. She knew she was going to marry Jason, and they were going to raise the perfect, happy family.

Her child, though not even an inch long, had changed her life, and in spite of who supported her, she wanted to keep it. No matter the gender or personality, the child would be raised in a home filled with acceptance, happiness, and unconditional love. However, her mother had other plans.

"It's alright, honey," Bethany heartened, "A little secret... I was a bit older than you when I had to do mine."

No one could know.

Agony oozed in crestfallen waves. Amanda's hands shook. She could hear her blood pumping through her body. How could she do this? It was against her religion. All of this. How could she fall so far from her faith? Hastily, Amanda put down the hanger.

"If you're going to act like an adult, then you have to make adult choices," Bethany scolded as she picked up the hot hanger and placed the cool side in her daughter's hand.

Salty tears melted down Amanda's rosy cheeks as she hugged her naked body in the bathtub. Never had she been so conflicted. Could she really do this? Amanda begged, but Bethany was obdurate. Her mother insisted this was the only way.

"C-can I at least go to the hospital?" Amanda whimpered. "Or take a pill?"

"That's illegal and a crime against our religion! You're too far for any pill, and father knows every doctor in town!" Bethany objected. "Anyway, the way people talk in this town, we can't risk anyone finding out. It would kill your father. Trust me; I've sanitized everything."

Premarital intercourse was immensely frowned upon in the Randall household, and her pregnancy was considered the worst form of malady. Cloaked in privacy, her secret was revealed only to Bethany as even Jason was unaware. Though her mother was deeply religious, she cared more about the shame a baby out of wedlock would bring to the family than her daughter's desires.

Furious and grief-stricken, Bethany condemned her daughter to Hell and insisted on an abortion. For the family's reputation and Amanda's ascension to Heaven, this pregnancy needed to be kept undisclosed, at least until it was completely eradicated.

Amanda was underage; she had no job or means of supporting a child. There was no father in the picture. Everything she touched morphed into catastrophe. Maybe her mother was right. How could she be a parent?

"I know it's hard," Bethany sighed. "Trust me, all the feelings that you feel right now, I have felt. You have to wait. It would be better for you and for the abomination inside of you. If you have this baby, it will ruin your life. Your father will disown you, and I'd have to support it. You don't want that, Amanda."

Amanda trembled; her wide blue eye welled with uncertainty. She had no idea if she could do the unthinkable. Jason had no clue of her pregnancy, and her mother clarified that she would never contribute financially or emotionally. Bethany threatened eviction from the home and ex-communication from the family. This was the only option.

"Please," Bethany begged. "My daughter, I have your best interests at heart. I just want you to have a future. To go to Heaven. I fear for your immortal soul… If you don't do this, Jesus will never forgive you."

Her shaking hand gripped the wire hanger tighter.

The blonde knew she would never stop wondering what her child would have looked like or even smelled like. She would never know whether it was an active little boy or a bouncing baby girl. However, she knew in her heart that this was wrong…but she also knew mother was always right.

"Go ahead," Bethany encouraged her.

Her breaths were short, and her eyes rolled into the back of her head. She had to do this. Amanda shoved the wire hanger inside of herself. It was a sharp, internal pain that burned all the way through.

"Argh!" Amanda cried out and ripped the yellow duckling shower curtain from the rings. It was like sitting on a flaming knife. Blood rushed from her, yet instinct told her she needed to go a little further. But she was not strong enough. Bethany placed her hand on top of Amanda's and supported her child the best way she knew how. She plunged the edge of the hanger further, then deeper. Amanda could feel it. Something inside her popped. A liquid warmth covered her body. Something inside of her had died.

Present Day

"I pledge myself to you," Amanda cried from her chains, "Brother Bainbridge."

Chapter 23: Fire Ring II: Amends

"There are heavenly bodies and earthly bodies, but the glory of the heavenly is of one kind, and the glory of the earthly is of another. There is one glory of the sun, and another glory of the moon, and another glory of the stars; for star differs from star in glory."
1 Corinthians 15:40-41

As the demon removed himself from the fallen angel, a flame engulfed her, and she shrieked inside of the boiling pool. Brother Bainbridge crept up to Neil. The demon was smug, and Neil could tell he was tired. Neil wrinkled his dynamic eyebrows as Diamond Love pushed him onto his massage bed. There was no use fighting. She forced him into a thick mud wrap. Diamond enveloped him so tightly in the silver cloth that he could hardly breathe. Neil bit his lower lip.

20 Years Ago

The day was almost perfect. Almost.

Neil had successfully tricked his parents into letting him stay home, broke into their liquor cabinet, made Victoria laugh, and, most importantly, lost his virginity. Nevertheless, he ended up vomiting into the downstairs toilet. He rested his head on the cool bathroom tile between heaves as his stomach was warm and contracted beyond his control.

Victoria was less than impressed. As a seasoned drinker, she held her liquor, and when Neil took an extended bathroom break, she knew exactly what was going on. Annoyed and disgusted, she refused to help her drunken lover simply because she had no desire. Regret bent her lips as she sat on the couch, and she listened to Neil hawk.

Suddenly a knock sounded at the front door. Victoria altered her outfit quickly, and adrenaline ran through her. She had been through this several times. Were Neil's parents back so soon?

Nervously, she inched toward the door and peered through the hole. There were three men outside, one was dressed in a suit, and the others were dressed in blue.

"Police!" the men shouted as they knocked.

The jig was up. Victoria hyperventilated and opened the door. His voice was deep and
burly, the man in the suit spoke with such command; it scared her, "Who are you?"

"V-Victoria,"

"Do you know where Neil Qin is, Victoria?"

She lifted her hand and pointed to the bathroom. The police scanned the scene and frowned with a repulse. There was an empty liquor bottle, used condoms, and the smell of sweat in the air. The man called Neil from the bathroom, "Neil, we have to take you down to the station…"

"I'm not going with you," Neil answered the door then yanked away drunkenly. "I haven't committed any crime!"

"It's not about you," the policeman sighed. "There was a gas leak at the church, a huge fire."

"What?" Neil's eyes grew three times their original size as he gasped. He dropped to his knees, and his stomach twisted up. He wiped his face with his vomit-covered shirt as he stuttered, "Where are my parents? Are you saying they're dead?!"

"We need to take you down to the station," the man closed his eyes regrettably.

"You're a fucking liar!" Neil attacked. "Is this how you do your job? To scare kids from drinking? Okay! I'll never drink again!"

"We need to take you down to the station," the policeman repeated as his colleagues surrounded Neil. The child broke down in tears. He tried to fight them off, but grief took all the strength from his bones. Realization crashed in like a wrecking ball: He had killed his parents.

Present Day

"I pledge myself to you, Brother Bainbridge," Neil cried as he was set aflame in a spiritual fire.

Chapter 24: Fire Ring II: Amends

"Then, I will draw near to you for judgment. I will be a swift witness against the sorcerers, against the adulterers, against those who swear falsely, against those who oppress the hired worker in his wages, the widow and the fatherless, against those who thrust aside the sojourner, and do not fear me, says the Lord of hosts."
Malachi 3:5

20 Years Ago

Ezekiel's mind was a cluttered mess. His father had drunk himself to sleep, and his mother chain-smoked through tears in the kitchen. Lauren's upper lip had been torn open, and her left eye was black, sealed with blood. How could he let him do that to her? That was his mother!

Ezekiel picked himself up from the stained tiles. He wiped his mouth clean of slobber and approached his mother. Save weak whimpers and the puffs of several cigarettes; she was silent for over an hour. Ezekiel was petrified and confused.

He crawled over to her and placed his head in her lap. Lauren's expression was stoic. Dead. She crushed the end of her cigarette and opened up a new box of Marlboro. Ezekiel needed her to acknowledge his presence; he hugged her legs as tightly as he could then looked up to her with a thirst for guidance.

"Get off me!" Lauren spat, flaming edge of her cigarette with an orange lighter. "Haven't you done enough?"

A vinegary sting of betrayal coiled around Ezekiel's tongue. Flabbergasted, he stuttered, "W-w-w-what did I do…?"

"We were happy before you," she announced. Lauren's glare was like an arrow to her son's heart. "I was happy before you. But, having a baby changes everything…"

Ezekiel pulled his sleeves over his fingertips; his eyes became overflowing saucers of briny water. "What did I do?"

"Don't cry!" The woman was exhausted and snapped with a cornered rat's panicked frustration. "You don't want your father to wake up, do you? You know what he'll do if he hears you crying."

"I don't know what to do!" he whimpered as he clasped his mother's knee tighter.

"Lauren exhaled a huff of smoke that made the entire room smell like ash, "Can you just not exist…?"

Apprehension simmered through his blood, and he released his mother's leg. Ezekiel fell backward so quickly he lost his balance. How could his own mother be saying this to him? What gave her the right?!

"If you don't love me," Ezekiel shouted, "I'll just run away and kill myself!"

Lauren rubbed her forehead as though her son's voice was a hammer to her skull. Carelessly, she retorted, "Go ahead."

Present Day

The memory was all too clear for Ezekiel; he remembered the first time he tried to kill himself. He was a child, but these memories would stay with him forever. Deep down, he accepted that the events in his life were all caused by him; yet in the past year, he realized that he could not control what happened to him or anyone else but only his reaction to the situation.

Ezekiel killed his father and abandoned his soul in Hell. It was just. However, he was sick of the guilt he held. There would always be a part of him that would miss Fredrick and maybe even love him, but Ezekiel understood;

fate was fate; it was part of a much grander design than himself.

This memory was just another lesson he had already learned. There was no need to see it again.

Inside a Distant Memory

"This is not my fault!" Ezekiel denied as his memories slowly seeped into his consciousness. Lauren's haughty glare was frozen in a lifetime of self-induced stress. Years of knowledge and experience entered the young boy's mind. This was a memory he had neutralized some time ago. He was stronger, and he could overcome this facile attack like a stroll through mild sunshine. Within seconds, he felt older, more prepared, and empowered. It was as though he was commanding a lucid dream.

His mother continued to smoke. His physical body wasn't tangible, but he could still sense something that felt like a heartbeat, though he had no breath. The angel pursued the area and noticed a creature was in the corner of the room. The gray man stood less than two feet tall. His naked body was so thin that his ribcage peered through, and he wobbled as though he could hardly hold up his broad bald head. Ezekiel accepted this variation of the Withers with eyes like black diamonds and a small mouth full of teeth shaped like broken glass.

Ezekiel shook his head to clear the fog; the demon seemed unaware of his consciousness. He summoned his strength and channeled it through his fingertips. As the death wave rolled through the room, he could feel his body transform. He was himself again. The Wither quivered but survived the blast. His mother continued to smoke as though unaware of the invisible warfare.

"Bainbridge uses Withers to clear people. God, I hate you things... How dare you hurt people this way," Ezekiel shamed the little bare creature. "Tell me about Brother Bainbridge, or I'll suck the life out of you."

The monstrous creature pointed his right index finger, and the tip of it glowed a soft white color. His lips remained still, but he communicated through telepathy, "We are the children of Beelzebub. We travel through his blood. We are Body Withers. We have a mission."

"What's the mission?" Ezekiel lowered his guard and asked; perhaps there was an antidote to all of this.

"Remove your humanity," the small charcoal being waved his glowing finger in the air. "So that you can become the Four Horsemen of the Apocalypse and the End of All Things can finally commence under Beelzebub's control."

"Okay," Ezekiel let out a tense, nervous breath, "Beelzebub, huh? Brother Bainbridge's other name?" Ezekiel's fingers were arched and ready to pounce. The name alone struck fear into his core, but he had to continue with his interrogation, "How do I kill Brother Bainbridge?"

The Body Wither caught his breath. He shook his head and waved his glowing appendage. "I will die for my leader! I cannot let you."

The brightness from the tiny finger grew so intense that Ezekiel was momentarily blinded. Ezekiel covered his eyes as the Body Wither transformed. From the demon's stomach cracked tendrils that whipped around like an angry six-legged octopus. A gray tentacle wrapped around Ezekiel's neck. The limb was so strong it was able to slam him into the kitchen sink as quickly as one would hammer a nail. Ezekiel was cut off from the air, and it felt like his head was going to pop from his body.

The angel channeled a death wave through his fingers, and the slimy limb recoiled, but as he fell to the ground, another appendage struck him across the face. Ezekiel slid across the floor as the demon wiggled its parts through the air. He attempted to attack, but before he could, a vine-like arm wrapped around his heel and pulled him to the ground.

Ezekiel was dragged to the demon's mouth, but before the Body Wither could bite, he took hold of its face. The small razor-edged teeth snapped like a piranha out of the water as it pulled him closer.

Face to face with this black-eyed monster and unable to scream, Ezekiel forced the creature's face away from his. The angel imposed all of his power into his fingertips. Life drained from the miniature man, and within moments his skin grew thin and black. Like fruit in a microwave, the Body Wither wrinkled and popped until there was nothing left but a pile of bubbling innards.

Ezekiel took a deep breath. He had won. However, the second he lowered his guard, he noticed he still was not alone. In the corner of his mind was a vision of pale yellow. The Horseman of Death stood in the shadows on his kitchen tiles. Ezekiel pointed and finger and shouted, "What are you doing here? I killed you already!"

"Whoa!" said Ezekiel as he awoke in a jolt. The psychic connection was disabled. Ezekiel suddenly found himself back in the Volcano Room, but he was completely clear of mind for the first time. He looked to his right. Neil, Aurora, and Amanda all had horse-shaped shadows covering their bodies. They burned in a spiritual fire and howled at the top of their lungs.

It took him a moment, but Ezekiel assumed the reality. Brother Bainbridge continued to shove his wrist into his mouth, but this time Ezekiel did not drink. Consciously, Ezekiel knew what he needed to do. He fought the urge to vomit the liquid he was fed and repeated, "I-I pledge myself to you, Brother Bainbridge."

Chapter 25: Can I Be Seen?

"I am so happy to see you all here!" Brother Bainbridge frowned. The angels stood in a line before their leader spoke. "The Hidden Eye demands a declaration of loyalty before they can trust you with your apocalyptic weapons, and you can fully become clear."

Aurora rubbed her wrists as the iron chains fell to the ground. She narrowed her eyes and snarled, "So, giving up our lives and staying here for weeks on fire and naked wasn't enough of a commitment?"

Ezekiel shifted nervously in his pale-yellow robe. He could tell by the void in their eyes that Neil, Aurora, and Amanda were not themselves. Brother Bainbridge. Beelzebub. Whatever the man's name had completely brainwashed his crew, his family. He knew that he was the only one who thought freely; but also understood he would never have a fighting chance against his teammates and a room full of demons. For now, he knew it made more sense to lie low and formulate a plan.

"They are rightfully suspicious," Brother Bainbridge continued. "You've given up your humanity, but you still have a few levels to transcend in order to become completely clear."

"What do we have to do?" Neil darted straight to the point.

Amanda twisted a curl of blonde hair around her finger and asked, "You're not going to make things any weirder than they already are, are you?"

"Before you can become Horsemen of the Apocalypse, we need you to prove your humanity is gone! The Hidden Eye has a small request. You must sacrifice one dear to your heart. To show your loyalty, of course. You know how these Brotherhoods are, always asking you to prove your devotion."

Ezekiel felt like he swallowed a boulder.

"That's a relief!" Amanda cheered, and her shoulder sunk with alleviation. "I thought it was going to be something serious; cuz as hard as I try, there are just some things I can't give up." She listed on her fingers, "Recycling, cheese, kittens, hugs…"

"I-I don't know if that's a good idea," Ezekiel stuttered as he pulled his yellow robes over his fingers and his nostrils flared nervously.

"Butterfly gardens… S'mores…" Amanda shut her eyes and concentrated as she continued her list.

"We must do what the Order asks, my friend," Brother Bainbridge warned. He reworked his sweater and grinned with a mouthful of yellow teeth. "They're asking for the life of a loved one and, of course, the traditional virgin sacrifice… with the still-hot blood of your victims. It ain't as hard as it sounds. But we do have a long day ahead of us. Murder your loved ones, my light will guide you to your virgin sacrifice, and you will follow it to the Mermaid Cafe. The Hallowed One has secured the area for us, and we will finally have you graduate from our program! Unfortunately for Hades, this is where we kill him."

"K-kill him?" Ezekiel recalled his last interaction with Hades or the Hallowed One as he was sometimes called.

The demon said they were related, pressed his sharp cane into his wounds, and told him about a hidden failsafe.

Ezekiel shuddered but tried to remain calm as Brother Bainbridge continued, "Of course. We've been friends for a long while, but I think it's time for him to go. I'd be a fool to hand power over to the Lord of the Death when I can just become him. Am I right?"

"Sounds easy enough," Neil agreed and planted his feet deep into the ground as if he were willing to kill anyone at the moment.

"Finally, we get to have a little fun." Amanda wrinkled her nose and shivered with an excited shrill.

"Could you be any more complicated? I don't even know who or where mine is. I don't care about anyone. How are we going to figure that out?" As usual, Aurora was annoyed; she placed her hand on her hips and examined her fingernails as she spat.

"I always have a way. Go along now," he announced with a wrinkled smile passed on his withered lips. Brother Bainbridge extended his finger, and the edge of it sparked silver light. He wiggled around the bright shimmer until it flew from his fingers and expanded like a heated puff of smoke. Once it was large enough, it surrounded the four angels.

Ezekiel shuddered in awe, and even Diamond Love's usually confident jaw dropped in frightened wonder. The terrified angel grabbed at his sleeves. Like the trapped air in a popped balloon, his voice burst from his body, "Stop!"

Though it was night, Neil's eyes had to adjust to the streetlamp's shine as it peered through the bedroom windows. The air was different again, lighter. He had no idea how long he had been detained in the Volcano Room, but his body had begun to get used to the shadows and hot grease particles that clung to the breeze.

This room was very different. It had pictures of cartoon characters on the walls and smelled of baby powder. As he noticed the mountain of stuffed animals piled several feet high, Neil recognized the room instantly. He peeked into the crib and watched his peach-faced son sleep. Zachary had grown large for a child a little less than a year old. He still had his father's chestnut hair and thick dynamic eyebrows.

Deep down, Neil always knew he lacked parenting skills. For most of his life, he took care of himself and expected others to do the same. He had other responsibilities. A baby was just a burden, a significant road bump in the path to the American Dream. There were times where Neil had regretted not being around for his son but knew the child would understand once he was older. Neil was going to make sure he had the best world for his son, even if he had to be absent to do it.

However, this was all in the past. Now, he felt emptier than ever. He lifted his hand toward his sleeping child and wondered: after everything in the past few months, was it really ever worth it?

"Neil!" her sharp shrill was easily discernible. The room was suddenly illuminated as Victoria stood at the entrance of her son's room. The blonde was wearing a white robe, blue silk boxers, and a yellow t-shirt. Her frosty eyes burned over lips that curved with such anger; it made her look much older than she was. "Look who finally decided to show the fuck up." Victoria placed her hand on her pockets and recoiled. "How the hell did you get in here?"

"You're always yelling!" Neil retorted before he delivered a telekinetic rush that lifted her off the ground by her throat.

Victoria kicked as she levitated and choked air. Her eyes bulged, and her skin reddened between huffs of breath. Had she gone crazy? Was she seeing all of this?

"Neil…. what are you doing?"

He nudged her into the light blue wall behind her so hard that the plaster cracked, and a framed picture of a cartoon mouse shattered. Victoria fell to the ground and grabbed her throat. She heaved in a desperate attempt to recover as Neil flattened her to the floor without a touch.

"I…" he paused for a moment. He had no idea what he was doing there. Brother Bainbridge had sent him to do something particular. Neil reached in his memory before he could finally answer, "I came here to kill our son."

"What?" Victoria's outburst took her mind off her own physical pain. "Don't you touch him! Neil! H-How are you doing this?"

"Does it matter?" he asked and raised an eyebrow.

"Yes!" Victoria shouted. "Of course, it matters!"

"No matter how hard you try," Neil's murmured, "you are never in control of fate. The universe is just a set number of insignificant occurrences."

Tears crept at the corners of Victoria's eyes as she was telekinetically held to the ground.
"How can you say that? You love your son! Fuck your dust-in-the-wind attitude! You have people who love you. We all matter!" Victoria yelped.

Neil wrinkled his brow, and the bones in Victoria's arms shattered like toothpicks. The angel's expression was empty, and his heart was numb. Her bawl sharp and ear-splitting as a siren. Zachary started to cry behind Neil's back as Victoria's appendages twisted up like earthworms plucked from the ground.

"Love doesn't mean anything."

"Do whatever you want to me, you bastard," Victoria managed to mutter through yelps, "but don't you touch my son."

"I don't have to touch anything to hurt it," Neil ended his rueful confession with a fist. Like a sheet of paper, Victoria's body crumpled into a mangled heap. Though her shriek was loud, he could hear every crack of bone and burst of an organ. One by one, they all fractured until finally, the screams stopped.

Crumpled and contorted, she was an unwound paper-clip in a pool of her blood. He had felt free. Freer than he had ever been. As he looked down at Victoria's dead body, an ashen taste entered his mouth. It was as cool and refreshing as water.

"Really?" Aurora growled through her clenched jaw, "It's you!" Aurora slanted her eyes as she glared down at the tall man. Thin white sheets covered his charcoal skin as he sat up in bed and watched television with a styrofoam plate full of Chinese take-out in his lap.

Biff was Aurora's ex-husband. She hadn't seen him since she left home. She was noticeably shaking, even in her sullen state. Memories of his regularly scheduled abuse seeped into her mind as she suddenly became angry with her psychic chauffeur. Why did Bainbridge's spell send her to this cheap hotel? With him? He was never dear to her heart!

Aurora's skin crawled. She pulled her red hooded robe over her knees and kicked the small wooden nightstand across the tiny hotel room. Biff was as unbothered as he was when she descended into the room in white light. With a sigh, he turned the television up and continued to eat his chicken and broccoli. Irritated, he announced, "I'm trying to watch this program if you don't mind."

"Okay," she proclaimed in disbelief. Aurora shook her head in doubt and annoyance. "I guess we're ripping the eyes out first."

"Two goddamn seconds!" Biff shouted, huffed, then retracted. He turned off the television and took a bite of the steaming broccoli, then admitted, "Fine. Let's talk; I'm mad at you."

"You're mad at me?" Aurora growled as she slammed her fist into her chest.

"Yes," Biff said boldly as he shoved his plastic fork into the styrofoam container. "Reality T.V and Chinese food are the best things about this time period, and you interrupted me." Biff stood from the bed. He was over six feet tall and muscle covered every inch of his torso. "Do you know how long I've been looking for you? You stole from me. Then you go off and become a Horseman of the Apocalypse. Without consulting me..."

"I'm not a Horseman yet..." Aurora protested as her jumbled thoughts began to contradict one another. "I still have to kill you and with your still-hot blood on my hands...sacrifice a virgin... Wait, how did you know about all this Horseman stuff?"

Biff uttered and stepped closer, "I've known you for many times, Gabriel, you've always been hot-headed, but never this stupid. My Gabriel, I loved you, I tried to save you, but you'd rather die for some lowly demon's cause."

"That's my angel name," Aurora stammered. "How do you know that name?"

The tall man pulled up his checked boxers as they fell below his long waist, folded his arms then chuckled. "Do you really believe Biff is my name?"

"You want to keep playing these little games?" Aurora said before she sucker-punched the tall man in the jaw.

"Is this even you? You are a little heavier than I remember," Biff teased.

"Then let me work off these carbs on your ass," Aurora suggested, then struck his face again. "You controlled every aspect of my life!"

She hit him again while he was stunned, then kicked him in the stomach. "I was trapped. You forced me to do things… Living with you was torture!" Aurora growled venomously, "Now I get to teach to a little thing about torture!"

"Gabriel, enough!" Biff called out in Aurora's mid-swing, then he was gone.

Suddenly, Aurora turned to see Biff towering over her. The bald, onyx-skinned man reached a concerned hand toward her, but before he could speak, she rushed him. Once she had him pinned on the wall, she snarled, "What are you?"

"Technically, I'm still your husband," Biff choked as Aurora pressed her knife up against his throat, "and I want my shit back."

"What shit?" she asked. Aurora's grip let up.

That's when Biff disappeared from her grasp. He appeared behind her and knocked her to the ground with a swift slap to the face. He revealed, "My weapon. You stole it from me, and you still have it; I'll beat it out of you if I must. That's what this was all about. Through pain… you find your true power." Biff scoffed, "Come on, black woman, aren't you gonna tell me how y'all suffer the most?"

Aurora mockingly pouted her full red lips, "You should worry about yourself."

She lunged at Biff but before she could strike, she was halted mid-movement. A familiar white light engulfed her, and for a moment, her movements slowed. Biff's eyes were red, and he moved with unrealistic speed as he tackled her to the ground.

Helpless and stunned, Aurora lowered her guard. As the smoky lights faded and time regained its average speed, she cried out, "How did you do that? That's my thing!"

"Give me my scythe," Biff exhaled. He was out of breath and coughed while he spoke, "Or I will take it from your dead body."

Aurora struck him in the face before she wiggled from beneath him. She scrambled across the floor and raised her fists defensively.

Biff shook his head, stood, then, with an irreligious grin replied, "Give me a kiss, baby; it'll be like old times."

"I've had a few upgrades since then," the angel countered as her eyes began to turn red.

However, he was a lot quicker than she was, and before she could release her temporal wave, he had a hand to her chest. Biff reached into her as quickly as he would enter into a pool. Her body vibrated as though it surged with electricity. For a few seconds, his hand was in her chest, and it sent vigorous volts of energy through her veins.

She was a portal.

Aurora screamed out in pain as Biff pulled a curved, green blade from her flesh.

She dropped to the ground and took a fist full of her robes. Each pulsing surge faded and there was no wound in her chest. Biff held the weapon above her as if in love with the sharp object. The elegant sickle was made from an emerald metal and engraved with Enochian symbols atop of a golden base. Stunning, the alluring razor called to her and, for a moment, sealed her in a state of awe. It was almost as though he tore her heart out, and all she could do was watch.

Disgusted, Biff turned from her and took a few steps. Aurora's eyes continued to turn red as she curled on the ground. "By the way, the name I've grown accustomed to is Kronos."

Her nostrils flared. There was no way she could allow Biff… or Kronos to ever defeat her again.

Kronos slit her face with the sickle, and Aurora's eyes flashed red. The time angel used her fingers to aim as she unleashed her time-altering blast through her squinting eyes. Kronos was covered in a glowing white mist. A bead of blood dripped from Aurora's nostrils; this man was powerful and took a lot of energy to paralyze.

She had to act fast.

From her previous encounter with the Horsemen, Aurora knew how this vanquish would work. Quickly she dashed to her frozen husband and ripped the marvelous green scythe from his fingers. Without hesitation, Aurora ran the blade across the man's throat.

Kronos gasped like a fish out of water.

The angel went blind for a moment as all the energy in the room ran to Kronos' throat. Like a black hole that ate up reality, the wound in his neck swallowed the contents of the room in a warped distortion. Aurora pressed her feet into the ground, and covered her face as existence contorted around her.

Bit by bit, time reversed.

Each period passed slowly at first, but as time rewound, days became seconds, then years crossed in instances. Before Aurora's eyes the hotel transformed backward through renovations. Decades of hotel remodeling melted away as construction workers, hotel patrons, and housekeeping aids scurried around like busy ghosts, forgotten fibers in the fabric of time.

Years dissolved backward in flashes. Aurora could hardly think as life spans felt like worlds passing through her. Before she could make sense of the changing scenery, reality would liquefy, and she would be in the same spot, but years, even decades prior.

Aurora took a deep breath of electric air. As the hotel began to deconstruct around her, the angel picked up the green blade. Through the rushing fissure, she could see Kronos. He crouched as the memories dashed around him and red juice leaked from his neck.

She was at a bar.

She was at a farm.

She was in the forest.

White.

As the glowing fog dissipated and Aurora's eyes changed to their standard color, Biff spurted blood like a sprinkler. She was in the present, back in the hotel. His body jerked on the ground like a wounded dog. In seconds, the man was dead. Aurora looked at the weapon in her hands. Even though she had never seen this powerful object, somehow, she felt like it was hers. Bewildered, she tucked the scythe beneath her robes as a white light opened from the ceiling.

Chapter 26: Am I Still Alive?

> "And the four living creatures, each of them with six wings, are full of eyes all around and within, and day and night they never cease to say, "Holy, holy, holy, is the Lord God Almighty, who was and is and is to come!"
>
> **Revelation 4:8**

As Amanda descended, white-hot beams burned her eyes, and while it faded, her delirium dwindled. Papier-mâché sculptures. Year-round Christmas lights. Pungent cat-litter follicles in the air. She was home. The blonde raised an eyebrow as she removed her black hood. Was Henry here?!

"Hello?" Amanda hollered before she paraded around the apartment. "Anybody home?"

"Oh," Olive said. She was in the kitchen, watering dead plants with a chipped Wonder Woman mug. The room smelt like hot honey, and Olive had already been drinking her signature glass of red wine out of a mason jar. She was pale, tired and almost appeared dead as she stood completely still for a moment. Her voice was hardly above a mumble, "Amanda, is that really you?"

"Oh my god!" Amanda shrieked. "Olive! I have so much to tell you!"

"You know," Olive turned from the shriveled dead cactus and muttered. "Maybe everything isn't always about you. Have you ever stopped to consider that something might be going on in my life? Everything doesn't have to be about you and your angel bull shit!"

"Well, you don't have to be rude," Amanda uttered, genuinely offended. She shook her head and tried to stable her rumbling thoughts, "I just thought you might be happy for me, that's all."

"And again, we're back on you!" Olive's green eyes scorched through her horn-rimmed glasses as she hissed. "I am so sick and tired of talking about you!"

"Well, fine!" the angel huffed. "Olive, how was *your* day?"

"Just forget it." Olive frowned. "Why are you dressed like that?"

"I lost everything. My clothes. My purse. My...Okay... Anyway, I've been wanting to ask you something for a long time now." With a tuck of her blonde hair behind her ear, she swallowed hard and asked, "I lost the house keys, somewhere, I don't know. Has anyone returned them yet?"

"No," the redhead's eyes slanted as she answered, "how would they know to come here with the keys?"

"Oh," Amanda flashed a confident smirk and replied, "I put our names and address on all of our keys. And I was always losing them, so I made multiple ones. Someone's bound to find it and return at least one of the pairs!"

"Wait," Olive's thin pink lips curved at their edges as she spoke with anger. "There are multiple keys to our home with our names and address on them all over New York City?"

"Great idea, huh?" Amanda giggled and patted herself on the back. "Just gotta wait for one of the good old citizens to return them."

"You fucking idiot!" Olive violently shouted. "You're no smarter than a bag of shit! This is all your fault! What happened to me is all your fault!"

The angel fell back and cried, "Olive, you're hurting my feelings!"

"More about you again!"

Amanda had never seen Olive this angry; however, there was a side of the angel that liked it. She recoiled, "Then I guess I'm going to have to just skip to the killing you part."

"What?" Olive blinked and asked in confusion, "Are you threatening me?"

"Boom!" Amanda belted as the dead cacti on the windowsill burst into flames.

Olive let out a perturbed cry and dashed into the living room. Amanda snickered and dragged her hand against the white walls and turned the paint black. Just as Olive had reached the front door, Amanda morphed the doorknob and locked into a malformed hunk of metal that shut them both in.

Olive turned to her while pure fear bulged through her eyes. She begged, "Are you really going to do this to me? Now?"

"Sure, why not?" Amanda tilted her head and asked. "Wait, since this is probably the last time we're ever going to see each other, we could have a little fun! Do you want to watch one more Disney movie? I'll let you pick the princess!"

"Fuck you," Olive spat.

Amanda propelled her finger forward, and Olive's face erupted in boils.

Olive let out a blood-curdling cry and fell to her knees. In a struggle of pure instinct, she grabbed her face. As the acid peeled the skin off her hands, she yelped in despair.

"Acid. It's a horrible way to die," Amanda admitted, shrugging as she skipped to the entrance. She transformed the doorknob back into shape and opened the front door, "I hope you left food for…"

The massive eight-legged cat hissed loudly behind her.

"Purrson!"

Chapter 27: Do I Have the Power to Change?

"Beloved, I urge you as sojourners and exiles to abstain from the passions of the flesh, which wage war against your soul."
Peter 2:11

Ezekiel's spirit animated his body like a bolt of lightning would energize a transformer. He reached around for something to touch and took in fistfuls of his familiar torn-up checkered bed sheets. Large brown eyes surveyed the room. Home. Everything appeared normal, except for it wasn't.

"Shit, shit, shit, shit," Ezekiel anxiously repeated as he sat upright and threw his knees off his bed. Brother Bainbridge had transported him home, probably to kill his mother. Ezekiel threw his legs over the bed; that wasn't going to happen. Neil, Aurora, and Amanda weren't thinking straight.

The Mermaid Cafe. He needed to get there to stop their accession. Ezekiel shook off the pins of nervousness that pulled at the edges of his pale yellow robe. Though this was not his usual attire, he was grateful for a moment, that he was at least wearing something. As he reached the front door, his mother called out behind him, "Ezekiel? You're awake?"

"H-Hi Mom," he stopped in his tracks and shuddered.

"Where have you been?" Lauren was generally concerned when she asked.

"I… will explain that the second I get back," he started, then inched closer to the door as Lauren followed behind him and stood in front of it.

Her arms folded, and her gaze narrowed, "I'm not letting you out of here without an explanation."

"Mom, please!" Ezekiel begged, then tried to step around her, but she was able to force herself into any path he decided to take.

"No! You don't get to do that!" Lauren shouted. "You don't get to show up out of nowhere dressed in a yellow robe and leave without saying a word! You are still my son! What the Hell is going on? Are you drunk? High? Son, are you on drugs? Did you join some sort of cult?"

"I can explain," he urged his mother believe. "But, I have to do it later!"

"You're not leaving this house until you tell me what's going on!" Lauren howled and planted her foot firmly into the ground.

"Mom, really? You still haven't figured it out?" Ezekiel reluctantly pulled his sleeves over his fingertips and expressed, "How do you explain the bloodstains in my clothes, the nightmares, the sneaking in and out of the house? Breaking the t.v. from across the room? You really didn't even notice anything? You couldn't even tell the difference between a Hell-spawn and your own husband! Why do you care now? Why bother with even being the least bit concerned with how I'm doing? Why don't you just go live in your fantasy world? I'll keep to reality."

"B-but I love you," her eyes welled with water as she tried to get her words out.

"And I love you too; I said I'll be back," the angel's voice became stern and heavy. "Now get the hell out of my way!" Ezekiel never spoke to his mother so harshly before, but the tension in the room had reached the maximum. Anxiety pinched at his spine; imperatively, he needed to get to the Mermaid Cafe. Ezekiel instantly regretted losing his temper and knew he would have to apologize for later…. if he had survived. Lauren sidestepped away from the door.

"I-I'm sorry…." Ezekiel stammered, "thank you."

Chapter 28: Contact with a Higher Power

Warm air whipped through the empty cafe as Cody and his friends awaited the call of the bird Clara spoke of. They were coming every day for a week, and he was beginning to run out of money. Tonight, however, felt special. Excited, Cody had come fully prepared. One of the benefits of being a super nerd was that he lived with his mother his entire life and could afford top-notch ghost hunting equipment. With his savings from his computer repairing job, Cody purchased an EMF Meter, a small device that was ready to pick up plasma waves and reveal the presence of supernatural creatures.

In his free time, Cody would often walk the streets with his favorite toy and scope out sites for his MeTube show, Modern Monsters: Men, Myths, and Mindlessness, so he knew a supernatural event when he saw it. Clara had been right. Cody discovered a rise in mystical energy in this small shop in downtown Manhattan. The Mermaid Coffee shop emitted the types of plasma readings Cody only heard of being found over consecrated burial grounds. This was the perfect space for an after-hours episode.

"Are we really going to break into the Mermaid Coffee for a story *again*?" Willie shrugged and glanced off at the full moon outside of the window. "I don't care what that doohickey says; we haven't seen hide nor hair of a ghost owl yet!"

"It's fine," Marshall coughed. "It's 2 a.m., and no one is out here. People are most likely asleep, away we're not going to steal anything, just a few minutes of filming this stupid ghost owl then we leave."

According to Cody's EMF meter, the Mermaid Cafe gave off particularly strong vibrations tonight, which meant they were finally likely to get a ghost on camera. Clara had always left the doors open with the alarms and security cameras turned off for her usual fifty-dollar fee. The lights were off in the cafe, so Cody switched the camera to night vision and surveyed the kitchen. Careful not to knock over any kitchen supplies, Marshall fixed his bowl-style haircut in the metal reflection of the oven. As Cody readied his camera, Marshall and Willie began with their standard opening.

"Welcome to Modern Monsters: Men, Myths, and Mindlessness!" Marshall whispered, "I'm Marshall, and I'm here in a downtown…"

"And I'm Willie!" the shorter reporter reminded Marshall of his role.

"Yeah, Willie is here too," Marshall cleared his throat before he continued, "I'm Marshall and I'm here undercover in a downtown Mermaid Cafe where there have been reports of a mysterious owl haunting the eatery after hours. Now, normally, my crew and I wouldn't just break into a corporate facility just for a story, but tonight the readings on the… U….P….S meter have gotten out of control."

Aggravated, Cody lowered the camera and snapped, "For the last time, it's called an EMF meter!"

Marshall's expression fell, and as he charged at Cody with anger, a sound from the cafe's lobby distracted him. It was the obscure echo of mutter that the three couldn't exactly understand. Slowly, Cody lifted the EMF meter from his pocket and turned down the volume as the small machine started to pick up energy.

Nervously, Cody followed the machine, and as the readings got stronger, he inched towards the lobby. With Marshall and Willie close behind, the trio peered through the window of the large metal door. Though he could hear voices outside the room, he could hardly see them. However, when he adjusted his camera, several figures came into sight. His heart dropped as he signaled for his friends to submerge deeper in their hiding spots. Breathlessly he zoomed in on the camera and gasped, "N-neil?"

The front door was open. Ezekiel had just arrived, and the scene was set just as he feared. The room was dark and filled with invisible spirits. A demon dressed as an older man in all black stood at the front of the coffee shop as the angels surrounded him in their long robes. Neil, Aurora, and Amanda all stood before four chained strangers. The virgin sacrifices? Ezekiel bit his lower lip. Brother Bainbridge was silent beside the Hallowed One as Ezekiel slowly entered the dim coffee shop.

Though Ezekiel could only count nine people in the room, he could sense that there were many more. Pulling his pale yellow sleeves over his fingertips, he walked to the center of the cafe. Though he had met the Hallowed One before, it seemed like his friends were just getting to know him.

"I'm Amanda Randall, pleased to meetcha!" the blonde beamed.

"Are you supposed to be like," Aurora sassed, then cocked her neck and placed a hand on her hip, "the evil Horsemen version of Lyssah? Because I have to warn you, I didn't get along with the original."

"The Hallowed One," Ezekiel gulped, remembering the demon from his battle with the Horsemen. Hades was the Horseman's advisor of the Apocalypse and rode behind them during the End of All Things. His wrinkled skin was a sickly pale yellow and covered in liver spots. Long hairs grew from his boney arched nose, and his gray teeth were small and pointed like a shark's. He wore a large black Amish hat above his thin elderly frame, a black suit, and a large gold ring with a symbol of an eye with a triangle around it. Ezekiel could never forget a character like this.

"The time has finally come. Cleared of your humanity, you are now ready to fully become the Horsemen of the Apocalypse. My Horsemen. You are now ready to take on the Devil's mark and your rightful place as enders of the kingdom." The Hallowed One spoke in a raspy voice. He looked toward Brother Bainbridge and nodded, "Thanks to you."

Every roll in his stomach jiggled as Bainbridge gave a hearty laugh, "It was nothing."

Ezekiel hyperventilated, and the scent of coffee was making him queasy. Traffic passed by, and their headlights chased away the shadows across the green mermaid logo in the small coffee shop.

He could feel the invisible eyes of the many spectators in the room. The demons spoke, but Ezekiel could hardly hear over the pound in his head and the pulse in his throat. He looked down to the cocoa-skinned teenager who was helplessly bound beneath him and almost joined her in tears.

"Well, I think it's mighty convenient." Amanda's cheer brought brightness to her solid black robe. She sat her red-headed virgin on the tile and admitted. "I used to work here… until I realized they don't support the LGBT..Q...R...STUWXY and Z community. We are all born equal. Anyone want some coffee? You wait right there, Gary!" She tiptoed across the large cafe and started to set up the machines.

"Gary?" Neil asked before he moaned disapprovingly. "Amanda, you brought a guy to the ritual? You were supposed to bring a virgin sacrifice..."

"He is a virgin sacrifice," Amanda walked behind the counter and started to turn on the heavy-duty coffee machines as she explained, "Gary here is only in high school and has been having a little trouble with the ladies. He is the captain of the chess club! He likes board games and ham sandwiches and old movies... I know, he sounds like a total catch… if only he were vegan… but that's why he's a perfectly good virgin sacrifice, Neil! And to say anything otherwise would be sexist!"

"Moving on," Aurora interrupted. "Can I have a grande caramel macchiato, double, low fat with low-fat whip cream and sugar-free vanilla syrup?" She paused. "What kind of bottled water do you carry?"

"You must have respect!" the pale elderly man in the black suit and round Amish preacher's hat bellowed. "This ground, young lady, is consecrated with the blood of Paymon. It possesses the ancient mystical energy necessary for your oaths. I am the Hallowed One! And I can show you how to do this ritual right! Worship and give praise to the dark lord..."

Was this really happening? Ezekiel never saw such a harsh stare in Neil's eye. Aurora and Amanda had captured weeping virgins as well. They were all under a spell, a trance or something! But why wasn't he? Why didn't Brother Bainbridge's jinx work on him? Was he going to have to face the entire room himself?

The Hallowed One cleared his throat and removed a golden cross from his jacket, "I had more help the first time around, but some fallen angels can be fickle nowadays...

Anyways, it's time for the sacrifice and your oath to me as your leader."

Abruptly, several chairs and tables pushed themselves to the side. Dressed in a white hood, Neil walked into space he had cleared for himself and instinctively announced, "I am Neil, I bring a virgin from the North."

Ezekiel couldn't breathe. This had to be a game. Were they undercover? If they were, he could not blow it now!

The Hallowed One placed a fine golden cross in Neil's hands, and he telekinetically pulled his victim to his feet. Amanda and Aurora watched unfazed as Ezekiel trembled beneath his yellow robe. How far were they going to take this? Horrified, he watched his former teammates strangle their victims into submission. Were they possessed? Why hadn't they escaped? Neil was so powerful. Even if he was the only angel that still thought straight, there was no way he would stand a chance against an entire room of demons and three fallen angels.

But he had to try.

Ezekiel pulled his sleeves over his fingertips, possibly for the last time.

"One moment, my friends," Brother Bainbridge interrupted. The grin on his face twisted with an unusual perverted curve as he announced, "I think there has been a change of plans."

"What is this?" the Hallowed One turned to Brother Bainbridge. "This is not how this ritual is supposed to go."

"Oh brother," Bainbridge admitted, "I confess, though highly un-neighborly of me, through clearing these little angels, I decided to keep them for myself. The Alpha Omega and the power of the Four Horsemen, rightfully they should belong to me."

"You know the scripture," the Hallowed One quoted. "It's rider was named Death, and Hades was following close behind him. They were given power over a fourth of the earth to kill by sword, famine, and plague, and by the wild beasts of the earth...'"

"Those old scriptures need to be updated," Bainbridge laughed. "After all, old rituals are never meant to be broken, but I think I'll make an exception this time." He cleared his throat and looked to the angels, "Continue."

Suddenly, Neil's expression glazed over with a deadpan countenance. He lowered his hand and, with an impassive tone, conceded, "I pledge myself to the Supreme Being."

Aurora was next. Her large brown eyes were glacial and empty while her face fell blank and she affirmed, "I pledged myself to the Supreme Being."

The iron chains in Amanda's hands dropped as well while Gary, her virgin, wiggled beneath her. She puckered her lips and dispassionately admitted, "I pledge myself to the Supreme Being."

Adrenaline shot through Ezekiel's veins, and he tensed as if he had just bitten into a lime. It was clear that the others were under Brother Bainbridge's control. The ancient demon quizzically watched Ezekiel and awaited a response. Nervously, Ezekiel revealed his fingers from his sleeves and was flummoxed; he shrugged, "I… am still undecided…"

Confused, Bainbridge angrily turned to the Hallowed One, understanding that he somehow got involved. Leading with his long black cane, the elderly man took a step forward, and with a crooked grin he announced, "I'm an Angel of Death. Of course, I have insurance."

Brother Bainbridge's eyes darted between the Hallowed One and Ezekiel as if he were scanning the surface of their minds. After a moment of silence, he finally threatened, "I control three-fourths of the Alpha Omega. Don't put it past me now; I'm the Highest Operating Psychic in the Western Hemisphere; I will annihilate them, so none one gets them. Surrender the fourth angel to me; there is no point…"

"Clearly," the Hallowed One mocked, "you underestimate the power of Angels of Death."

Without another word, the man in the Amish hat threw his bident across the room like a javelin. Ezekiel raised his hands in defense, but he was struck through the chest before he knew it. For a moment, the hot spear blinded him but as the weapon passed through his body and pinned to the ground, Ezekiel realized his soul had moved with it. Struck through the chest, Ezekiel's astral body was fixed to the tile by the sharp cane and forced to watch his physical body as it stood from the ground.

Stunned, Ezekiel watched his body brush itself off and huff in exhaustion, "Wow… anyone got a cigarette?"

"Welcome back, Mors," the Hallowed One greeted. "Nice to see you again. How do you feel?"

"It's good to be back." Mors examined Ezekiel's body for a moment. "Like my other outfit better… but this body… you were right; I could feel that it was holding back."

"Well, now here's your opportunity," the Hallowed One announced, "life and death, Horseman and Angel, the two halves of the coin finally merge. Show us what you can do…"

Lights flickered across the green, and white coffee menus as the heat rose and advertisements shook from the walls. Ezekiel grabbed at the magical cane that impaled him; however, his incorporeal hands passed right through the mystical device. Seconds later, the room stabilized, and Bainbridge was twelve-feet tall. Surrounded by bees he arched his long pointed fingers and narrowed reptilian, yellow eyes. Like a rattlesnake, he hissed through black lips and aimed a hand at Mors.

However, as reality started to distort around Mors, his nostrils flared with intensity. Ezekiel was helpless as he watched Mors operate his body like a villain in a costume. Suddenly, Mors' palms were on fire. He lifted them waist-high as his eyes filled with a red light. Unlike Aurora's eyes, Mors' pupils glowed with a hint of green and purple.

Red, green and gold beams of energy shot from his back like flare guns. The light show covered the room in an aurora australis. Ezekiel tore at the stick that bound him to no avail as he could hear the four victims in the room squeal under their gags. In his spiritual form, Ezekiel could not feel most temperatures, but as the windows fogged around him, he could tell the temperature had considerably dropped.

Being a celestial entity, he had no physical form, yet he could feel pain and the anxious pins that pushed inside him as he could sense spirits entering the room. Like floating foam from a bubble machine, spirits flooded the cafe. Popping in and out of sight, the tadpole-like specters stormed the shelves of packaged coffee grinds and knocked the designer mugs to the ground. They shattered the fluorescent light bulbs and turned on the industrial coffee machines.

Unplugged blenders spun while kitchen utensils collided with floating furniture, pastries, and cookware.

The flickering rays of light form wing-like beams on Mors' shoulder blades as he levitated, three feet off the ground, his palms still held out flat and on fire. Ezekiel hadn't seen a show like this since Neil's overpowered outburst at the park. Was Mors tapping into Ezekiel's potential?

As ghosts shimmered around him, Ezekiel was finally able to get hold of the bident; however, it still would not budge. He looked to the Hallowed One, who enjoyed the Northern Lights show as hues from the australis borealis lit up the giant Brother Bainbridge and the crashing coffee shop around him.

Abruptly, a sinking feeling bubbled into Ezekiel's gut. It was a harrowing sensation he instantly recognized. He glanced over to the large basket of plump green apples placed by the cash register and winced in horror. As if placed next to an invisible heat, the fruit wrinkled and blackened. Energy poured from the produce until they were left decayed and cored while the wave of energy took over the room.

"No!" Ezekiel cried out as he watched the four bound virgins quiver beneath the shadows.

Like the apples, their skin thinned and darkened. Irritated veins bulged through their flesh as life was sucked from them. Years of aging passed over until their bodies shriveled motionlessly under the reflecting red and green lights.

Bainbridge winced slightly before a crooked smile crossed his face, "Well done."

The twelve-foot-tall demon burst into thousands of frenzied insects that took off in an explosion around the room. The tiny bees disintegrated in mid-air in less than an instant, showering the cafe in motes of black and white ash.

Ezekiel closed his eyes and tried to return his spirit to his body, but the natural pull he felt when his consciousness entered his flesh was blocked. No matter how hard he tried to activate the power he had gotten comfortable with months ago, there was suddenly an invisible wall that prevented its use.

"W-why can't I go back?" Panicked and confused, Ezekiel's transparent jaw dropped as Mors landed on the ground and extinguished the flame on his hands. Immediately the lights from his back faded as his eyes returned to their brown hue.

Amanda, Neil, and Aurora seemed to wake from their trances.

Possessed by Death, Ezekiel's flesh had pale yellow eyes and rotted gray teeth. Mors controlled his new body like an expert puppeteer. He pointed the finger at Ezekiel as the temperature in the room boiled, and the air was saturated with substantial energy.

Anxiety no longer had any physical effects on Ezekiel. Sweaty palms and speedy heartbeats were replaced by sharp tingles, hollow voids, and intense gravitational pulls that yanked from every direction. The Horseman of Death had taken over his body, and he was powerless to return it.

Ezekiel had never felt so ultimately alone.

He was empty, and his form was flimsy. Echoes of gentle splashes whispered in his eardrums, but there was no running water. The sound of a river rumbled off the walls. He wanted to cry, but a stranger operated his tear ducts. There was no one to help him, and he began to feel weak.

As agitation ate his energy, the pellucid ectoplasm that his consciousness consistently emitted waned. The suction that yanked on his soul devoured all of his strength until his form vanished from sight.

Chapter 29: What more can I do?

Cody watched as Marshall and Willie trembled behind the kitchen doors. Before anyone could speak, Marshall dashed over to Cody and snatched the camera. He cleared his throat and gazed into the lens, "I don't know what we just witnessed, but this has been brought to you by Marshall Donkin!"

"Marshall!" Cody objected and seized the camera from his co-host and hushed him, "This is serious! We just saw some sort of… supernatural battle!"

"We're about to get famous!" Willie cheered. "Keep filming…"

"Guys," Cody frowned and admitted, "I'm not sure about this..."

"You don't want a cut in the millions?" Marshall arched his eyebrows and asked. "That's fine with us! I thought this was 'our show'. You're the only one who really knows how to work the camera and do the editing! You're not going to make us lose another lead, are you?"

Petrified, Cody agreed, "Fine."

"The other Ezekiel was more fun." Amanda frowned and waved her hands in front of the demon who controlled Ezekiel's body. Death's pale yellow eyes narrowed in frustration as he stretched the muscles in his newfound flesh. Moonlight spilled through the shattered windows and lit the area just enough for the five to see each other.

"Shouldn't there be someone we should be killing?" Aurora snarled.

"No, no, no," the Hallowed One adjusted his black Amish hat and wagged his boney finger side to side as she scolded her. He slowly walked past the destroyed coffee shop holding a heavy steel two-pronged spear that he used as a walking cane, "I told you about fighting."

"I thought I was the Horsewoman of War!" Aurora declared and pointed at the withered old man dressed in all black.

"Not yet. Not until you sacrifice those virgins and sign a blood oath. Only a Clear can do that. There is more to becoming Horseman than you understand." The senior cracked an empty grin full of only a few corroded sharp teeth.

"We understand enough," Neil answered for Aurora. "How do we break the Fifth Seal?"

"Sweetheart, do you really have no clue?" he chuckled. "Why do you think I did all of this? Creating you is how I broke the Fifth Seal." The painfully thin man laughed hysterically, "I know my years precede yours, but do you really have no idea?"

"Before you start, let me know if I should get something to eat," said Aurora, rolling her eyes, "or is this going to be one of the quick three and a half-hour speeches?"

"Do not mock me! Do you think this wasn't all fated?" he bellowed as Neil, Aurora, and Amanda gazed at him with curious eyes. "The Fifth Seal is you becoming the Horsemen! We all knew how this would turn out! You see, I am much more than just your Hallowed One; before the fall, I was one of the original Seraphim of Death! I shaped

Tartarus! I was the bane of life! The End of Existence! Every human alive and dead feared the name *Hades, Anubis, Mictlantechuhtli*! Those who spoke my name shuddered in terror!"

Amanda frowned sympathetically as the veins in the Hallowed One's neck grew large with anger. She cooed, "Aw, I'm so sorry, Hades, I don't think you're that bad..."

"I'm a coldblooded monster!" Hades slammed the bottom of his cane on the floor in anger. "And as a Horseman of the Apocalypse, you will address me as your 'Hallowed One'; your advisor and leader!"

The blonde lowered her head in shame and apologized, "I'm sorry."

"Don't be you, weakling," the Hallowed One warned. "We must make sure the Fifth Seal stays broken. Just a few housekeeping rituals before we can move on to the Sixth Seal."

"Which is?" Neil asked.

He tipped his Amish hat and started to sing, "'And I beheld when he had opened the sixth seal, and, lo, there was a great earthquake, and the sun became black as sackcloth of hair, and the moon became as blood.'"

The decrepit man walked up to Amanda and tapped her on the forehead with his knuckle. As she fell to the ground, he continued his song, "'And the stars of the heavens fell unto the earth, even as a fig tree casteth her untimely figs when she is shaken of a mighty wind.'"

Aurora cringed as he got near, but he quickly tapped her on the forehead as well. Instantly the angel fell to the ground in unconsciousness. The Hallowed One sang even louder as he pranced around the cafe, "'And the heavens departed as a scroll when it is rolled together, and every mountain and island were moved out of their places. And the kings of the earth, and the great men, and the rich men, and the chief captains, and the mighty men, and every bondman, and every free man, hid themselves in the dens and the rocks of the mountains.'"

The Hallowed One tapped a willing Mors on the forehead. With the support of his thin, two-pronged cane, the elder walked closer to Neil and paused. He took a deep breath before he finished, "And said to the mountains and rocks, 'Fall on us, and hide us from the face of him that sitteth on the throne, and from the wrath of the Lamb: For the great day of his wrath is come; and who shall be able to stand?'"

A bright white light filled the room, and within a second, the angels were gone. A small brown and white owl flew across the room and dropped tuffs of fluffy feathers. Cody lowered his camera as his friends silently cheered. It was challenging to film in the dark, but he was sure that he had actual footage. He shoved the device into his knapsack while Marshall kept watching on the Hallowed One who remained. Marshall ducked from behind a large countertop and quickly tiptoed over to Cody, "Did you get everything?"

Cody smiled sarcastically and retorted, "Did I just become Cody the Magnificent?"

"W-was that a supernatural initiation?" Willie asked.

"We're gonna be rich!" Marshall whispered a shout.

"Or dead," a weak voice wheezed behind them. Hades was so old he trembled as he stood. The frail senior grabbed his heart as if his pain was not only emotional but physical as well. "Oh, drat, there are bats in the lighthouse."

"Sorry, dude..." Willie apologized and raised an eyebrow.

Hades narrowed his gaze.

Willie's insides tore up in brutal knots.

"Silence, boy," Hades spat.

Gallons of blood rushed from his mouth, a horrific eruption, and Willie fell into a pool of his own fluid. Hades switched his gaze to Marshall as he trembled in fear. Before the metal-mouthed man could speak, red liquid streamed from his eyes. He choked on his exploding insides and dropped.

Hades turned to Cody, who was pointing a flare gun at the demon's head. The red curly-haired boy's dumbfounded eyes were large and filled with the salty liquid. He could hardly hold the weapon in his hands, and he struggled to stay conscious simply.

Hades smirked pompously, "Poor boy, you really think that can stop me?"

"N-no," Cody managed to whisper through jolts of fear. Slowly he aimed the flare gun at the fire alarm. "But, I know that if I set off the emergency security system, the cameras g-go to a corporate live feed all over the planet…"

The elderly man chuckled a bit as he leaned in toward Cody and responded, "No worries, I'll be seeing you soon anyway." He turned on his heel and ended the conversation. Slowly, he walked away and whistled an old tune as he swung his cane in a circle and vanished in the darkness.

Chapter 30: Can you hear me?

"I believe that these extra-terrestrial vehicles and their crews are visiting this planet from other planets... Most astronauts were reluctant to discuss UFOs. I did have occasion in 1951 to have two days of observation of many flights of them, of different sizes, flying in fighter formation, generally from east to west over Europe."
Major Gordon Cooper

Cody had locked himself in his room. Beads of water soaked his orange bangs and glued them to his forehead. The man was exhausted; he had run the entire way home. He threw his glasses on his desk and fell into his chair. Tears fought their way out of him like the puckers of a tired engine. Were they really dead? Should he call the police? How would he explain the scene?

The redhead shook uncontrollably and tried to hold in his cries so that he didn't wake his mother. He quickly found that he had sobbed so much that his neck and the collar of his sweater were soaked with sorrow and sweat.

This was all real. Cody had always believed, yet he never expected to encounter such a hot scene. As a constant reader with an interest in the otherworldly, he learned all about demonic experiences. However, he never thought it would indeed happen to him. He tasted the chalky presence of pure evil and survived. His body refused to stop trembling.

Marshall and Willie were dead. They were his only friends, and now he was alone. What was he going to do? Cody wiped his tears. Hades threatened him. Could it mean that he was next?

No.

In the memories of Marshall and Willie, he refused. He opened his laptop and typed in "the church on Rector Street."

Scolding rays attacked the exhilarated, overflowing crowd from a cloudless sky. The dry breeze carried dust through the countless, tiny American flags that the assembly proudly waved. Penny-sized horse flies hunted through the sweaty and diverse audience but failed to distract the men and women as they jumped on the backs of one another in anticipation.

Every corner of the National Mall was garnished with red, white, and blue decor. This was the first time in Washington, D.C., for many of them, and standing beneath the stairs of the Lincoln Memorial was a humbling experience. A large podium covered in expensive red cloth and ribbons were at the top of the massive staircase, and behind it, twelve respected politicians patiently waited in line before flailing flags.

Frantically the supporters recorded every aspect of the experience and even photographed the massive murder of crows that loudly tore apart trashcans and dragged rotten garbage throughout the immaculate lawns only yards away.

Respected videographers aggressively cheered among the many and readied their cameras as the massive security guards made room for two figures to enter the stage. Fran Miller Robinson was a wall of flesh, thin but full. Her broad, masculine shoulders bulged through her black suit jacket as she smugly crossed the stage with the grace of a tortoise. Her delicate, ear-length, brown hair caught the hot winds as she shook the hands of the respected officials around her. Under her red rectangular glasses, her beady eyes refused to blink as she regarded the crowd and made space for her husband.

A roar of applause echoed through the hallways of the memorial as Nathaniel approached the podium. He was a tall, attractive man who always wore an expensive black suit with a red tie. Nathaniel showcased a mouth full of perfectly crafted veneers every time he smiled. The crowd repeated his name, and he waved bashfully.

"Thank you," he cleared his throat and fixed a wrinkle in his suit. "Friends and family, that's who all of you are to me; thank you for coming out on this scorching day and supporting me throughout my political career. It really is an honor to stand before you today.

As many of you know, my family has been involved in politics for generations now. We've been mayors, governors, and senators. Our love for this country runs so thick in our blood that even at the young age of eighteen, my daughter, Caroline Robinson, asked me if she could join the army. Now imagine my mix of emotions! As a proud father, I raised a beautiful, responsible, and intelligent young woman who loves her country; but she was also my little girl, and I didn't want to see her get hurt! Caroline also proved to be a determined young woman because though I selfishly pleaded for her to stay, we both knew it was where she needed to be. We kept in touch, of course. We wrote letters and called whenever we could. She was only a few months overseas when she wrote me this one letter in particular..."

Nathaniel's brown eyes welled with stubborn, stagnant tears. In a moment of reflection he adjusted his tie, "I had just gotten home at the time, and Caroline expressed not only how much she loved and missed me but how proud she was to call me her father. She said that she believed I could make all my dreams come true: An end to monopolies, a fair universal living wage, international unity, the progression of not just one country but the entire human race! That was the last I've heard from Caroline. They lost all communications with her troop...Her body was never found. It is because of her that I have the strength to call you here today before this historical monument to announce my candidacy for president of the United States!"

Nocturnal insects feverishly bounced atop the murky water in search of food. Quick mating calls echoed through the blackness as their secret war began as it did every night. Rattling trees spread pine scents, pollen into the air, discarding brittle twigs into the dark lake. Moisture refreshed the breeze and sprinkled glittering dew across the stone bridge when lightning bugs suddenly dimmed their lights.

The air ran colder.

Aquatic beetles were silent. They avoided the abrupt heat rising in the center of the lake. A dark blue light flickered beneath the waves, and bubbles boiled to the top. In an instant, the entire surface of the lake blazed with an intense sapphire flame so hot it dried the dew on the bridge. From the middle of the gurgling disturbance, a man desperately emerged. He had only a second to take in air as the blue fire rushed out of the water and to his skin. Frantically the flaming man screamed as he lunged for the shore.

Relentlessly he swung his arms through the water until his bare toes pushed into the muddy, black soil. The icy embers slowly died off the ivory skin of the muscular man as he gasped, now needing a breath. Phanuel narrowed his round blue eyes in frustration. At first, the transition from hot to cold felt nice on his wet naked skin, but as earthly consciousness settled, physical awareness increased.

He needed to get dressed.

Chapter 31: What is theFate of all Heroes?

"And when he had opened the fifth seal, I saw under the altar the souls of them that were slain for the word of God, and for the testimony which they held: "And they cried with a loud voice, saying, How long, O Lord, holy and true, dost thou not judge and avenge our blood on them that dwell on the earth?" And white robes were given unto every one of them; and it was said unto them, that they should rest yet for a little season, until their fellow servants also and their brethren, that should be killed as they [were], should be fulfilled.

Revelation 6:9-11

Phanuel quickly found that he hated descending. Though he charged through the dingy alleyways with the agility of a caffeinated ape, he felt almost claustrophobic in his heavy sack of flesh. His vision, once boundless, was dimmed. Colors were dull, and he soon realized that some did not exist at all. Scents were less potent, and the more repulsive odors in the back lanes, like piss and filth, caused physical reactions he never felt before.

Sound now had volume and echoed in his eardrums like tiny explosions. He struggled to hear the wings of the moths as they danced toward street lamps but could not block out the blaring sirens of police cars. The pain was an annoying handicap that lingered far longer than it used to. In his original form, he possessed so much brilliance that mortals burned in his presence.

He was disabled, sensitive, numb, and vulnerable but had a job to do.

He traveled the empty roads in a limited six-foot hunk of meat and bounced shadow to shadow, unsure of where he was headed but charged with a divine trust. Phanuel was careful to avoid busy streets until he reached the metal gate of the closed store. Through the iron fence, he could vaguely see the stock of weaponry the shop displayed and was disappointed at the inferiority. He scanned the vacant store before snapping the lock and lifting the gate just high enough to slip under.

Phanuel's eyes adjusted to the darkness, though they never needed to before. He was surrounded by dozens of blades of various cuts and origins. The long, heavy, two-handed Chinese sabers hung beside two smaller Celtic swords while the sickled Egyptian khopesh hid behind glass. Over the millennia, he had enjoyed watching humans and recognized most of these swords and maces.

With a keen sense of smell, he identified each weapon's age and metal, and with a careful vision, he studied their sharpness and strengths. Phanuel's inspections were swift but thorough, yet the store was stocked with inventory.

"Freeze!" the voice echoed through the shadowed corners of the shop. Two police officers aimed their pistols at the muscular back of the stocky powerhouse. Phanuel strapped a small round shield to his left arm. Then he buckled a leather belt that held a leaf-shaped, double-edged bronze sword to his naked waist. He fisted his free fingers around a long, steel spear with a double-edged, bronze blade at its end.

The men dressed in black advanced toward Phanuel and cocked their pistols before ordering, "Lay down the weapons! Now!"

Phanuel sighed, disappointed with his newly discovered shortcomings. There was a time when he would have sensed them blocks before they approached him. His ringlet brown locks dripped with sweat and recoiled as he turned to his attackers. How did they know he was here?

He rolled his powder blue eyes over the several cameras that hung around the shop. Silent alarms, of course. He had forgotten they had those.

Without fear Phanuel spoke with a grimace, "Do not stand in my path, for I am an angel of the Lord."

"I said 'put em down!'" the first cop responded.

"You interfere with God's command," Phanuel narrowed his brow when he snarled. "Turn away now, or you will regret it."

"What are you on? That 'nectar' or whatever those kids are calling it? Where are your clothes?" the second officer asked as the first released a warning fire into the air.

"You're wearing them," Phanuel threatened them as he slowly pointed the copper, tear-shaped edge of his spear toward the officers.

Chapter 32: What is the Fifth Seal

"When the Lamb opened the fourth seal, I heard the voice of the fourth living creature say, "Come and see!" I looked, and there before me was a pale horse! Its rider was named Death, and Hades was following close behind him. They were given power over a fourth of the earth to kill by sword, famine, and plague, and by the wild beasts of the world."

Revelation 6:7-8

Electricity blazed throughout his essence like rushing comets, but they began to cool down as they came together. Suddenly the pain stopped, and he was able to see again. Ezekiel was right where he started, at the doors of the coffee shop. The Mermaid Cafe was just as it had always been, full of light and people.

The howling abyss haunted Ezekiel with an echoing ring that was silenced as he adjusted to his surroundings. Desperately, Ezekiel grabbed at his translucent form. He was still a ghost, but the coffee-addicted pedestrians ignored his presence. He examined his spectral fingertips, which faded in and out of sight.

When his eyesight adapted to the brightness in the room, he noticed that the coffee shop was, actually, not just as he left it. Oxygen moved in gentle, glittered waves. The light then bounced off the air, and coffee machines like sunshine through prisms.

The warm aroma of honey spread like a pollutant from the white, six-petalled flowers that had grown from the tiles, walls, tables tops, windowsills, and ceiling fans. Ezekiel's jaw dropped as he kneeled to one of the strange plants. Instantly, he recognized the flowers from art class: asphodels. Unnaturally, they sprouted everywhere he looked.

"But Mom," Cody protested as his mother snatched a steaming paper cup from him, "it's tea!"

"Chai tea!" Sylvia Goldenblatt spat before she guzzled the piping hot liquid in a single gulp. "You have to think about caffeine. I know you're just acting out because of what happened to your friends, but a caffeine overdose is not the answer."

"I told you not to talk about my friends," Cody objected. "I'm here doing research!"

"You cannot tell me anything until you pay your bills, and even then, you still have to respect your mother!" Sylvia snarled. "Do you think I could ever talk to my mother like this? *My mother*?!"

A muddy brown light covered Cody's skin, and it twitched with anger. The glowing man stormed toward the exit, and though Ezekiel nervously waved, Cody passed right through him then out the doors. It felt as though someone had grabbed Ezekiel's insides and shaken them.

"Can anyone hear me?!" Ezekiel's holler echoed off the walls, but the world around him was deaf to his pleas. This had never happened to him before. He was weak; Death must have cursed him. He was helpless and needed to go to the nearest graveyard, where he could recharge.

Like the coffee shop, the rest of the city was the same but had a few slight yet strange differences. Ezekiel pulled his sleeves over his fingertips and hesitantly wandered the streets of Manhattan. The mystical asphodels grew ubiquitously. They were resilient and bloomed regardless of surface or placement.

Citizens were blissfully unaware of the white flowers that sprouted purple buds atop busses, inside subway cars, and below taxi cabs' tires. Ezekiel was also invisible but almost preferred it that way because, in this world, emotion was tied to animated energy that bounced off people in glowing fields.

The radiations varied in color and size, but all sparked with excitement whenever its host got upset. Ezekiel had never felt so utterly alone in a strange world. His destination was more than an hour's walk away, but he had no other travel option.

Pedestrians shone in black and red lights as they argued on their cellphones and pushed through one-another. An angry teenage girl with three nippy chihuahuas rushed past a mother with twin blonde toddlers and shouted obscenities.

When the golden-haired caregiver raised her middle finger in retaliation, a moving van wholly covered in the milky asphodels sped through. A rush of the thick honey scent made Ezekiel nauseous, as though he had swallowed an entire sappy sweet gallon of syrup in a single gulp.

He fell to his knees and tried to shake off the constant coils of queasiness. Before he could steady his mind, an immense flame crackled in front of him. The blaze rocked in fluid motion as if dancing to the beat of a slow song. Heat licked Ezekiel's ectoplasmic flesh, and for the first time since he had been exiled from his body, he felt warmth and comfort.

His history with mystical fires made him suspicious, but the hot current was so alluring he reached out his hand to touch it.

"Wait!" a voice called.

Just as his spectral digits came close to the bonfire, he was tackled to the ground by a young, transparent woman. Her form was more substantial than his, and she was more robust as she pinned him to the ground. Her cat-like eyes rolled with frustration as she scolded, "Don't touch that! You some kind of A Minus?"

"Y-you can see me?" Ezekiel squirmed from underneath the Asian American ghost. "Wait. Why?"

"Because," she paused awkwardly then slowly rolled off him before she answered, "it'll take you to Hell! Or

Heaven, which is even worse because there they make you pretend."

"Well," Ezekiel disagreed and raised a confused eyebrow. "I don't know about all of that..."

The fire cracked with an angry burst of energy and surrounded them. Within seconds the road around was ablaze. A burning storm engulfed the passing cars, streetlights, and the women who argued on the sidewalk. Though nothing was harmed or affected by the supernatural explosion, Ezekiel could feel the dangerous intensity fry his ectoplasmic essence.

"Your fault! See what you did?" she scrambled to her feet and rebuked him. "Now we must phase through the fire!"

The ghost girl hurried toward the wall of flame, but Ezekiel quickly rose in objection, "I can't! S- something's wrong with me! I haven't been able to use my powers since—"

"Maybe A Minus..." she said, running back and taking Ezekiel's hand, "...was an overestimation!"

Ezekiel had no choice but to follow the apparition's long black hair, who guided him through the inferno. With her touch, he was numb to the heat and could pass through

unharmed.

Chapter 33: Will I Ever Return?

"When the Lamb opened the fourth seal, I heard the voice of the fourth living creature say, "Come and see!" I looked, and there before me was a pale horse! Its rider was named Death, and Hades was following close behind him. They were given power over a fourth of the earth to kill by sword, famine, and plague, and by the wild beasts of the earth."
Revelation 6:7-8

"Hurry!" the long-haired ghost floated ahead of Ezekiel; effortlessly, she passed through people, brick walls, and fire hydrants, levitating over newsstands and garbage cans as they hurried through the city. Ezekiel struggled to keep up with this agile spirit as she quickly navigated through the obstacle course of human traffic and street signs with ease.

Unable to control his powers in his weakened state, Ezekiel trailed behind but was determined to follow the only person who could see him. He could hear the young woman shout in the distance, "Do you want Purgatory to catch you? Keep moving lazy bones; we're almost there!"

Running was different when Ezekiel had actual legs, but energy was energy, and he barely had enough to hold his molecules together. The hazel-eyed phantom stopped at the doors of the downtown pet store, Pet World Markdowns. Impatiently, she waited for Ezekiel to reach her side before she revealed, "I used to work here."

She grabbed Ezekiel's hand, and they passed through the glass doors littered with advertisements.

Pet World Markdowns was an embarrassing assembly of mismatched tags, misplaced merchandise, and over-crowded, unclean cages. Ezekiel could no longer smell the same, but he saw the various stenches rise from the dirty tanks with dead fish and the filthy litter boxes kept with dingy kittens. The store was filled with people, and the loud animals desperately cried out for help as their empty bowls went unnoticed.

The spirit threw her waist-length raven hair backward and seemed to relax. She announced, "The only animals they know how to care for are dust bunnies. They kill more animals than they sell. All the death that happens here clouds Purgatory, but we can't stay here forever."

"P-purgatory?!" Ezekiel asked, wrinkled his brow, and halted in mid-step. He fisted his hands in frustration and felt an imbalance in his form. Suddenly, the birds stopped chirping, the dogs were quiet, and even the fish ceased to swim. All the beasts in the room fell silent. They watched Ezekiel with terrified open beaks, lips, and jaws. Behind him in the showcase of smaller rodents, the hamsters jumped into their wheels and frantically raced away but got nowhere despite their efforts.

"Not this again! Why do I always have to be the one to travel to other dimensions?" Ezekiel exclaimed. "First Hell now Purgatory! Why can't Neil visit another world?"

"Simmer down!" the hazel-eyed girl instructed. "These animals have malnutrition to worry about; they don't need you scaring them into an early grave!"

"Who *are* you?" he asked. Ezekiel eased his temper as the spirit trudged off. He followed her as she started to open bags of pellets and spill them into empty bowls of starving rabbits and guinea pigs. "And how can you do that? I haven't been able to touch anything since I got to Purgatory."

"I'm Zakuro," she glared at him from top to bottom with a judgmental grimace and answered, "and apparently,

I'm a lot smarter than you. We're not in Purgatory; we're being chased by it. We're in the Asphodel Meadows."

Ezekiel's brow wrinkled in confusion. He inquired, "Where?"

"The Astral Plane, the Elysian Fields!" she yapped as if she was already annoyed with his company. Zakuro brushed away the long black strands of hair that covered her eyes, "Why do you think you can see people's auras? You know, it's the space between life and death, Heaven and Hell, this world and the next; are you slow?"

"Don't answer." Zakuro pressed her index finger on Ezekiel's lips and answered for him, "Now I gotta go. You'll just get me caught by Purgatory."

Just when the young girl dressed in all black turned from him, Ezekiel reached out behind her and begged, "Please, don't go! It's not what it looks like. I-I'm an angel!" Ezekiel nervously stuck out his chest and cleared his throat before revealing, "The Angel of Death and I go by the names Uriel and Suriel. I'm one of the Alpha Omega too!"

Zakuro instantly stopped. She folded her arms and turned around with a scowl of suspicion, "If you really are an angel, why do I feel your presence fading by the second?"

Ezekiel sighed and admitted, "It's a long story."

"I'm dead," Zakuro confessed with a smile, "it's not like I'm going anywhere..."

Amanda lifted an eyebrow as she watched the Horseman of Death light a cigarette inside of Ezekiel's body. Though Neil, Aurora, and Amanda had all changed, their souls' core remained, while the soul that inhabited Ezekiel was utterly foreign. Death inhaled his cigarette deeply as the five supernatural beings routinely gathered in the Mermaid Cafe after dark.

Aurora and Neil continued to the main floor of the Mermaid Cafe, where tables and chairs were pushed out of the way to make room for the sacrifice. It had taken the four all day, but because of the delay, Hades had instructed them to amplify their ceremonial offering with a future Saint rather than a handful of virgins.

"This is my third time I'm doing this ritual," Death complained as he yanked the sacrifice behind him. "Hopefully, this one sticks."

"Just remember why we're here," Hades warned.

Amanda rushed over to the bounded young girl and frowned beneath her black cloak, "Death… she's a future Saint; you have to remember not to be careful."

The Horseman of Famine elevated her open palm, but there was neither spark nor glow, and the innocent victim remained unharmed. Amanda looked at her hands and questioned her abilities, "Hey, what happened to my powers?"

Stunned in bewilderment, Amanda turned with just enough time to see a double-edged spear fly toward her. Just before it hit, however, the weapon floated off its target. Neil was ready. With his eyes, he guided the spear and buried it into the wall behind him. Beside him, Aurora twirled her sword in her hand with a mastery that now came naturally to her.

She giggled as she recalled, "I can see the future! Did you really think I wouldn't know you were coming?"

"I knew they would send you. Are you here to clean up the mess?" the Hallowed One admitted as he tapped his two-pronged walking cane on the tile beneath him.

Slowly, Phanuel revealed himself, and he inched out of the shadows. The stocky angel was dressed in the ill-fitted navy blue uniform he stole just hours ago from the policeman, but he was armed with weapons he was more familiar with. He held a double-edged sword in his right hand, and attached to his right arm was a small shield. Begrudgingly Phanuel beheld his familiar with utter disdain as he spoke, "Disgraced, fallen angel."

"Welcome to Earth, Phanuel," Hades greeted, "is this your first time?"

"Forsaker," Phanuel triumphantly divulged, "you have committed crimes against the allied Heavens. By order of the Divine, I command you to surrender!"

"Oh, I haven't been to Heaven in a long time," Hades respired. "Locked out, you know… but a nice responsible daddy's boy like you… you wouldn't happen to have an extra Halo for me, would you?"

"Kneel in the name of the Lord!" he commanded. With the nimbleness of an Olympic acrobatic, Phanuel rolled over the cappuccino machine and swung his double-edge sword at Death's head. The skilled soldier only slightly missed as Neil levitated a coffee table at him. However, Phanuel thrust forward and smashed the wooden furniture to bits with the shield attached to his arm. He was hurled back several feet but landed in a graceful stance while his shaggy brown hair fell in ringlets around the thick stubble on his chin.

"We know what you have," Neil informed him as he pointed an accusing finger, "the entryway into Heaven. Give us the key to the Elysian Gates, and we'll make your death quick."

"Look at yourself," he muttered. Phanuel's sky blue eyes narrowed with exasperation as his lips coiled with disgust, "I used to call you brother, Michael. I knew you had the soul of a human… but now you stand a lowly demon! You mustn't give in to your grief! Fight your impulses, or die where you stand!"

"I'm sorry," Neil bitterly disagreed. He lifted his ivory bow above his head and fired several white arrows into the air. "Have we met?"

Though the arrows were powered by telekinetic guidance, Phanuel could block them with his shield or spin away from their assault. The blue-eyed angel smashed his shield into Death's face and, as he dropped to the ground, and headed toward Aurora.

Her eyes started to heat up, and her pupils became crimson, but before she could launch her time-altering attack, Phanuel waved a hand that shimmered a ghostly blue. Aurora's powers were instantaneously shut down. He flipped toward his spare and pulled it from the wooden wall. The well-armed warrior reeled to Amanda then placed his palm on her forehead.

Reality ripped around his fingers, and tints of blue flickered around the disruption. Amanda closed her eyes and dropped to her knees in fear as the angel refused to let go of her face. He narrowed his eyes in concentration and, in a fit of exhaustion, threw her to the ground with a forceful shove.

She lay there, motionless for a while… then lifted her head as she smiled.

"Was that supposed to do something?" Amanda used her glowing digits in a gleeful attack and set fire to the tables and chairs around Phanuel. "Oh, Angel of Exorcism, I guess you're losing your touch."

Even though the angel had stunted her powers, Aurora still had the skill of a warrior. She struck at him with her sword, and Phanuel raised his weapon in defense, but his talent soon fell short of the perfection of the Horseman of War. With a swing of his wrist, Neil telekinetically tossed Phanuel across the room.

He stumbled backward until Death approached him with focused precision. Phanuel felt the lifeforce drained from him and clawed into the ground in total horror.

"You're no match for all of us!" shouted Neil, and swung his hand above his head as the entire room shook. With a tremendous psychic wave, Phanuel was hammered into the brick wall behind him.

"You can nullify abilities, you can exorcise demons, but you are less than what you were," Hades laughed. "I think it's time for you to kneel."

So this is pain, Phanuel thought as his eyesight flickered on and off like the light from a flashlight with dying batteries. It was worse than he had imagined. He went numb. Muscles and joints burned. There were cuts and bruises on body parts he had yet to discover. But he had a duty; his grasp tightened around his shield. Heaven entrusted him with this task, and he could not disappoint, especially not during the whispers of a civil war.

"I am the Angel of the Lord!" Phanuel took a deep breath and announced. Like sparks of electricity, one by one, the veins in his eyes grew bold and blue. Once his eyes were recolored entirely, they began to glow. The angel stood from his knees, and rays of light floated from his back like two blue ribbons in the breeze. Phanuel spat through chattering teeth as blood started to drip from his ear, "You want the key?"

The glowing angel lifted his hands above his head as a golden ring appeared above it. Just as it seemed, he quickly snatched it from the air, hoisted his mighty bronze sword, and smashed the above Halo. The sparkling aura surrounding the Elysian Key promptly faded, and Phanuel tossed the cold, brown piece of metal to the ground. It was his only way home, but it needed to be destroyed. He pounded his shield with his sword and let out a deep battle cry.

"Great, now what?" Aurora snarled.

Neil turned to Amanda in anger as he noticed the prisoner had fled, "Weren't you supposed to watch the sacrifices?"

"I'm sorry, but everything got so exciting!" The blonde shrugged and apologized as she noticed the young Saint they spent all day tracking down was at the side of the warrior angel.

"We are never going to get this done!" Aurora shouted in frustration.

Red and blue beams penetrated the shadows of the cafe as fire truck sirens blared. Though Phanuel could not see the four's faces, he could feel their eyes burn with wrath. He knew they had the upper hand, but he had to admit there was some sinful pleasure in not letting them get what they wanted. Phanuel took the future Saint into his arms and escaped into the darkness.

Chapter 34: Do you remember me?

> "There is nothing permanent except change."
> **Heraclitus, 4th century BC**

A gentle cricket song hummed alongside the soothing sounds of rushing water and the tiny squeaky noises that clanged from the rusty hamster wheels. PetWorld Markdowns was void of humans, but it was still bustling. Zakuro had turned the pet store into a safari. With their cages opened, chinchillas, doves, rabbits, guinea pigs, parrots, lizards, cats, and dogs transformed the collection of neglected jail cells into a peaceful community where each species shared in the straightforward enjoyment of stretching and having a decent meal.

"I feel like I'm in a Disney movie," Ezekiel muttered nervously as he watched goldfish spin with delight while Zakuro sprinkled fish flakes throughout aquariums. "Do you do this every night? Who cleans up?"

"Who cares?" Zakuro responded and rolled her hazel eyes as she brushed her pin-straight, charcoal hair from her face, "The animals have to be taken care of. They're the only ones who see us without judgment."

Ezekiel watched the pretty young dark-haired girl as she placed birdseed in her hand and fed two small white and blue parakeets. The astral plane was much different than the normal one; Ezekiel could not only sense the joy from the animals, but saw it with his own eyes as it radiated off them in blue tints. He had to ask, "Can people see you too?"

Zakuro snarled, "When I want them to. But I don't need self-satisfaction."

"Remember everything I told you? There's someone that I'm trying to reach," Ezekiel finally figured he'd pop the question. "She's a nun. She might be able to help me, but only if she could see me... of course..."

"I can't believe you're an angel," the female ghost put her hands on her hips and moaned, "supposed to be one of the best ones at that, and you don't even know the general mechanics of this world?"

"I told you I was reincarnated so that I would have a human soul!" Ezekiel protested. "I don't remember anything from my angel past."

Zakuro took Ezekiel's hand and led him into the center of the store. The almond-eyed ghost was rough and forceful, so when she sat down, he immediately followed suit. Rabbits heartily bounced around her, excited for attention as she ignored them and solemnly spoke, "Apparently, there's a lot you don't know about this plane. Most importantly, it is the same as our old world, cruel, dangerous, and stupid. We're just at a different frequency."

"Like when you're driving around and listening to the radio," she rolled her eyes as though she was annoyed with the conversation before it had even started. "You could get the same station on a different channel, but one may have more fuzz than the other. Asphodel Meadows is a lot more dramatic. Every action, emotion, and relationship has its own color, energy, scent, and frequency. We can just see them, these auras, in the astral plane. If people just learned how to channel their energy, they wouldn't have so many problems."

Zakuro continued in her monotone utterance, "Here, you just think about it and it happens; energies are living things and they manifest themselves. That's why when people are negative, bad stuff always happens to them."

"Or I'm negative because bad stuff always happens to me," Ezekiel admitted while a shy smile curled at the edges of his lips.

"You can't be seen because you don't want to be," she confessed. "No one cares for these animals. These animals see me because I want to make a difference. Why are you here?"

Ezekiel paused for a moment then questioned sarcastically, "Do you think you're deep or s-something?"

"I'm no, Mr. Miyagi, but I'm good at reading people. I think I can help you get back into your body," Zakuro announced and lifted a large brown rabbit into her arms, "if you can do one thing for me."

Ezekiel readily nodded.

"Protect me," she pulled the bunny in close to her as she whispered, "No Heaven, no Hell, no Purgatory or fields... I just want... to exist." He took a step forward, but she stopped him from speaking with sharp words, "Don't ask questions, just do it."

Ezekiel reluctantly agreed.

"You can start by," Zakuro held out the fluffy brown creature in her arms, her voice as cold as ever, "petting the rabbit."

Chapter 35: Do you know me?

Phanuel thought the rain's purpose was to refresh the earth, but as the heavy droplets carried blood from his various cuts, all he felt was a disappointing sting. It took every ounce of his physical strength not to scream out in pain as Phanuel squirmed at the foot of the church doors. Flesh injuries were poles apart from spiritual wounds, but they had their own debilitating effects. With both fists, the angel slammed into the double doors that were engraved with religious entities. Earthworms crawled up from the soil and drowned in puddles as the coarse smells of mud and blood stained the air.

The throbbing numbness made it difficult for the warrior to think, but he was sure he was in the right place. He implored, "Let me in; it is your duty! I require aid!"

Inside the disheveled remains of the use-to-be-church, Lyssah huddled with her fuzzy owl. She wore a shapeless gray smock littered with holes and covered with food. Her knotted silver hair was twisted up into a bun, and her pale, tired eyes were shut tight in aggravation. A large elephant gun rested between her knees as she shook her head and repeated chants in Latin.

Since the church had shut down, Lyssah and Stolas were utterly alone. She refused to rebuild because, at this point, it was unnecessary. The nun ignored Phanuel's calls while she listened to the forceful droplets of rain as they splattered across the rooftop.

Though her concentration was unyielding, the lights flickered, and she could no longer let Phanuel's persistent knocks and screams go on. Just when the older woman cocked her gun, the massive circular stained glass window above the doors shattered. Stolas escaped into the air as shards of crystal showered the beige tiles under the nun's peach slippers. She raised her gun and aimed, but she was unsure she could pull the trigger when her target came into focus.

Red fluid seeped from the angel's lesions. His eyes were glowing a bright blue, and two sapphire rays sprung from his back and flapped hopelessly like giant, broken wings. With thick arched eyebrows, Phanuel reached out to Lyssah and cried out in a voice that filled the entire room, "Lyssah, sister, have you completely abandoned all your lineage? Have you truly betrayed our Father?"

Lyssah cocked her pistol again. She narrowed her dull eyes, then lowered her gun, and murmured, "No, I just grew up."

Phanuel spat angrily through bleeding gums, "Help me, Lyssah!"

Stolas landed on a brass candelabra behind the priestess. The pitter-patter of the rain echoed throughout the church as the wind carried howls and water through the broken window. Slowly, Lyssah dropped her weapon and approached the bleeding angel. She threw his arm over her shoulder and lifted him onto a wooden pew. Without saying a word, she fetched a first aid kit, then wiped Phanuel's cuts with an alcohol swab.

"Your wards are getting weaker, it could be a while, but I was able to sense you, my sister. It'll only be a matter of time before others can too." As she cleaned his wounds, Phanuel winced through beads of sweat, but he managed to ask, "Do you know why I'm here?"

"Because you sit before me," Lyssah supposed. "Big, bad Michael almost ate you all up. No time to fix you; I'm supposed to be securing this place! There's no protection, no cloud here! It's unsafe. Apparently, anyone could get in."

"I was asked to come here," Phanuel grunted, "and unlike you, I am an obedient—"

"Slave?" she finished his sentence as she roughly bandaged his wounds.

"And what have your choices gotten you, oh Angel of Free Will and Self-Determination?" he asked then slouched in the pew to ease his pain as he looked her up and down. "Oh, Goddess of Madness. Nothing but your dismissal from the order! Repent! This holy ground looks shameful! You smell! The other seraphim know that you've lost your mind. Lyssah Rhamiel, Sister Tabbris, why would you allow yourself to look so old?"

"I don't mind my appearance," Lyssah affirmed, "I had to grow up. It is my choice."

"But we were created to serve and protect!" Phanuel protested.

"Don't get excited. I protect!" Lyssah insisted. "There's plenty I do to keep order."

"You are in danger here." Phanuel cleared his throat as he warned her, "You know she's still out there, Athena. Killing the older ones. We've been keeping watch."

She sat speechless for a moment. Lyssah had many difficulties controlling her emotions, but very rarely was she unsure of what she felt. Reluctantly, she pulled up the sleeves of her smock and revealed the several small Enochian symbols she carved into her skin, "Just because I haven't been around doesn't mean I'm not with you. I still see you. My poor, sweet brother, I can feel you."

Phanuel feverishly twitched in his seat. He hated surprises, and this one was under his nose for over millennia. In shock, he responded, "You were kicked out of the Angelic Order. How could you still hear us?"

Tears filled the old woman's eyes as she coldly murmured, being sure to draw out every word and fill it with resentment, "Because I hear everyone."

"We never assumed your empathic abilities were so," Phanuel paused before he spoke, "acute."

"Soon, the next Seal will shatter, and the earth will break. There will be many deaths. Powers of Exorcism aren't enough," Lyssah warned him. "We must remind them of who they were."

Chapter 36:: Are we switching the times?

> "At his best, man is the noblest of all animals; separated from law and justice he is the worst."
> **Aristotle, 4th century BC**

The air was as thick as wool. Though Ezekiel had no physical body, there was a nauseating coil that rumbled in his core. His vision shook uncontrollably while reality rippled around him like heat waves as he sat cross-legged on the floor of the pet shop. Zakuro was surrounded by frightened animals that chirped and cowered, but she showed no concern for their fear. Her hazel, almond eyes zeroed in on the ghost, and her mind remained focused. However, Ezekiel failed to match such concentration, dropped his head, and caused the fizzing energy around him to dissipate.

"Do you not want to see your body ever again?" Zakuro screamed with the relentless aggression of an obsessive-compulsive football coach. "You weakling! Every ghost has access to her bones! Remember what I taught you, and you won't be seen! Come on A Minus, stop being lazy!"

The angel's lips twisted in frustration. Over the past few days, he had gotten to know Zakuro very well, and he knew it would be pointless to combat her militancy; after all, she was a good teacher.

Reminded of his training, Ezekiel focused on releasing his essence into the air. Once he heard a distant howling, his vision started to wiggle. His fingers clawed outward as he felt electricity jolt through his being. Though he gritted his teeth, the physical stress release no longer applied, but it helped him to recall how it felt to have flesh.

Without warning, a pang shot through his soul. Unlike having a body, Ezekiel felt pain throughout his entire shape rather than just the injured limb. It felt like he was gutted and plunged several thousand feet into the cold, rocky earth. The pressure popped his ears and manipulated his sight.

When the whirlwind of compression ended and his vision cleared, he found himself in the center of Fort Greene Park. The ghost instantly recognized the nature reserve from the massive cylindrical monument beside him. The Prison Ship Martyrs' Monument was a stone tower dedicated to Americans who died in British ships; Ezekiel had visited it many times, but he had never seen the park in this condition. The six-petalled star-shaped flowers covered the vast open fields of grass and trees in white. They breathed purple pollen that quickly diluted into the crisp night air. Ezekiel almost considered it beautiful if it hadn't been so eerie.

Suddenly he felt queasy. He knew his body was close. In the distance, a shining ball of light shot across the field like a falling star would travel the sky. As the figure rushed closer, the rumbling reverberation of thunderstorms echoed throughout the park, and a glowing doe sped toward him.

Ezekiel was stunned by the white deer's magnificence and grace. The spirit's golden antlers struck from its head in radiant bolts of lightning and lit up the area around her with every bold auric crack.

The beast stopped before Ezekiel; its large black eyes bulged in fear. Trapped by an unseen force, the white doe kicked its legs hopelessly as it floated into the air. Within a split second, the glowing spirit was punctured with six long white arrows. Neil, Aurora and Amanda, and Death appeared beside the golden hind as it fell to the tall stone tower, sprinkled in white flowers.

Panic pumped through Ezekiel's form, and his instincts urged him to hide; however, he realized as Zakuro instructed, he was only invisible when he convinced himself of it. The beast cried out in agony as it hung from the air like a white pincushion dripping in red wine. When the four were close, the doe burst as easily and spontaneously as a balloon would pop. Ruby plasma melted over the Four Horsemen's robes as they removed their hoods.

With blood on her face, Amanda addressed her team, "That felt better than I thought it would!"

"I told you," a shaky voice murmured from the darkness. Hades, the Hallowed One, crept from the shadows dressed in his usual all black and a large round Amish hat. "The blood of a Ceryneian Hind has invigorating qualities. With the loss of the virgins and the promised Saint, the sacrifice of this holy spirit should be enough to commemorate your ascension as Horsemen."

"Finally!" Amanda cheered.

He smiled with a mouth full of gray teeth and pointed with a boney finger as he spoke slowly but cheerfully, "Yes, bathe my warriors. No, I won't make a mistake this time; you four are now endowed with the power. And tomorrow, you will shatter the Sixth Seal."

Ezekiel could hardly believe his eyes as Death removed his pale yellow hood and licked the hind's blood off his fingers. Ezekiel had been through a lot in his life but never had he felt so utterly violated. It was alien to watch his body move and talk under the control of another. He wanted to throw up, but his spectral form was unable. Who knows what disgusting acts Death could be doing in his rented flesh? Ezekiel wanted his body back; however, he knew that he wouldn't be able to do it alone.

Epilogue

"You're not powerful enough yet!" Zakuro warned as she followed Ezekiel down the empty streets of Manhattan. The dawn sun-kissed the old gum covering the sidewalks and licked the crumpled-up newspapers and fast food wrappings that blew through the wind. Ezekiel loved getting up this early and enjoying the morning, but with no feeling in his body, the sun failed to warm him, and the air was stale. The asphodel's honey pollen mingled with the red-orange scents of garbage cans and old food. Rats ruled the streets this early, and upon their diseased backs rode familiar little creatures Ezekiel held a personal abhorrence for.

Withers mounted the rodents like tiny naked jockeys. They cheered and snapped their pin-like sharp teeth as they clung to the fur on the animals like parasites. Ezekiel shivered; no doubt the demon population was growing, and these bald, nude disease-causing fiends were proof.

He hiked through the large shut metal gates and up the stairs of the Lord is Our Savior Church. Ezekiel ignored Zakuro's advice and continued to march toward the large wooden front doors of the church until she appeared before him and shouted, "You're still a flimsy little spirit, you know? I could probably stop you!"

"You can try," Ezekiel confessed, "but I have to get to Lyssah. I think I can get her to see me. She's not like other people."

"We can't risk it!" Zakuro disagreed, then folded her arms, "What about Purgatory? We have to get back to the pet shop before it smells us!"

"After I told you what I saw!?" Ezekiel shouted. "They're possessed! I have to go!"

"You're a fucking idiot!" Zakuro ranted as he stepped around her and continued through the massive oak doors. Reluctantly Zakuro followed, "And so am I..."

It was like he entered the church for the first time. The holy place of worship was a complete mess. Broken wood and tile covered the floor, and spider webs clung to the ceiling. Dust collected on the glass shards that lay where they fell from the former window above the mighty engraved doors.

Lyssah stood on a ladder and whispered to herself as she slowly painted large alien symbols on the chipped walls with a complex concoction of blood and rare materials. Stolas was atop her shoulder and watched as Ezekiel charged through the aisle.

Excited, the owl flew from the woman's shoulder and onto the altar. Stolas hooted loudly as Ezekiel anxiously approached, "You can see me. Can't you?"

"Has the little birdie finally taken flight?" she asked. Lyssah swung down the ladder with the agility of a woman much younger. Her tired, teal eyes were like arrows that shot Ezekiel in the face. "Come now, are you finally ready to be seen?"

"Lyssah!" Ezekiel cried out. He was hit with a joy that was missing for months. He reached toward her for a hug but stopped short as he had trouble controlling his tangibility and exhilaration, "I'm so glad you can see me! I've had such a rough couple of days!"

"Yes, yes, yes, I can feel you," Lyssah repeated as she blinked, "hungry. Starving. All mixed up in the underworld with Persephone and her pomegranate seeds… You mustn't eat them. You must never eat them, no matter how they may tempt. Now, now, now." The older woman soothed her rambling by changing the subject, "Speak, speak, speak, you busy, loud bird's nest!"

Zakuro snarled as Phanuel entered the room.

"Archangel Uriel," Phanuel called; the stocky angel was now completely healed. He wore the same ill-fitting police uniform he had stolen only hours before. Around his wrist was a round red and black shield, and around his waist, a leather belt held a bronze sword. His muscles swelled as he walked with a steady pace and respectfully bowing before he spoke, "It's an honor working with an angel of your ranking. I will assist in any way I can."

"O-okay," Ezekiel nodded nervously and asked, "Lyssah, who is this guy?"

"A future memory," Lyssah answered quickly.

"Right," Ezekiel referred to the ghost who shyly hid behind him, "this is Zakuro, she helped me, you know... be seeable."

"Who?" Phanuel asked and cocked a perplexed bushy eyebrow.

"She's a ghost. She's right here," Ezekiel thought, then frowned as Zakuro shook her head. "Maybe she's on a different frequency or something...?"

"Shut up..." the apparition muttered as she ducked behind Ezekiel.

"Messages are meant to be delivered!" Lyssah demanded impatiently.

"S-sorry!" Ezekiel apologized. "I actually do have something to say. When we defeated the horsemen, we became them, and when I astral projected out of my body, Death the Horseman somehow took it over! Now Aurora, Neil, and Amanda are planning on breaking something called the Sixth Seal by causing an earthquake, I think?"

"Do you know where?" Lyssah jittered apprehensively as Ezekiel shook his head in affirmation.

"Now we have a thousand soldiers... We have to stop the galloping."

"How? I can hardly f-fight like this," Ezekiel stuttered.

"No way!" Zakuro raved while she made her way to the door. "I didn't sign up for a fight against Super-Powered-Angel-Horsemen of the Apocalypse. You'll have to do this alone!"

"Okay," Ezekiel muttered as the female ghost slipped through the door.

"Whatever," she farewelled and phased through the exit, "good luck and good riddance."

"I will help," Phanuel announced valiantly then stepped forward. "We must kill our brothers before they break another Seal."

"No!" Ezekiel objected.

"Shh," the nun stomped her foot, "I can hear the breeze across the ocean. I feel the thirst in the forests. I know the secrets that others can't hear. Like the Alpha Omega, all Four Horsemen are required for the circle to exist. You need only to clear one Horseman to break the bond. However, neither of you has the power to defeat them. But I can help."

"You're going to leave the house?" Ezekiel asked as the older woman knelt in front of a wooden pew.

"I know of a better way," Lyssah asserted and reached below her shabby gray smock. She revealed a crooked knife that rusted with crud and dirt. Readily she placed her left hand on the bench and cut down through the bone in one swift motion. Ezekiel screamed, then shivered when the sound of the knife repeatedly dug into wood as she was sure to separate all of her stringy tendons and skin.

"Goodbye fingers," she whispered with melancholy. When the bloody deed was finished, she dropped the knife, and the sound echoed throughout the noiseless church.

Ezekiel covered his mouth in horror; he was nearly speechless, "Oh Lyssah... What did you do...?"

The old woman picked up her detached appendage and let it bleed in her right hand for a moment before she passed it along to Phanuel, "With this key, any heart will be open to you."

"Thank you, Sister, I will treasure it," he sternly accepted, and Phanuel took the dripping hand. He was unfazed by the brutal act but grateful for Lyssah's sacrifice. The angel tucked the detached fist into his suit jacket and looked toward Ezekiel, "Take me to the seal."